"Sit there and don't speak!"

The disheveled man ordered Philippa to a bench in the innyard. "It may interest you to know, madam," he said through his teeth, "that the horses you so high-handedly demand have only narrowly escaped burning to death; and this innkeeper, whom you fondly imagine to have been bustling about to obey your orders, has in fact been fighting a fire in the stable for the last three hours."

When the fire had subsided, a half hour later, the man returned to where she sat. Philippa sought to apologize but he cut her off, saying, "I've sent a stableboy ahead to 'The Partridge' to obtain fresh horses. Your coachman's just re-harnessing yours to drive there. The new team will be waiting for you when you get there."

"I am so sorry," Philippa said breathlessly. "Thank you so much. I've been behaving abominably."

The man laughed. He looked down at her lovely, ingenuous face beneath the modish bonnet of celestial blue.

"Don't feel guilty," he told her. "Don't think about it at all." Then, as much to his surprise as Philippa's, he put his arm around her and kissed her swiftly and expertly.

Astonished, she struggled in his arms and he set her free abruptly. "May I wish you a safe journey?" he said with a slight bow. "Perhaps we shall meet again—in Lo

Your Warner Library of Regency Romance

Philippa

Katherine Talbot

WARNER BOOKS

A Warner Communications Company

WARNER BOOKS EDITION

Copyright © 1979 by Katherine Ashton
All rights reserved.

ISBN 0-446-84664-3

Cover art by Walter Popp

Warner Books, Inc.,
75 Rockefeller Plaza,
New York, N.Y. 10019

Printed in the
United States of America

Not associated with
Warner Press, Inc.,
of Anderson, Indiana

First Printing:
May, 1979

10   9   8   7
6   5   4
3   2
1

Some who once set their caps at cautious dukes,
    Have taken up at length with younger brothers:

              . . . .

There's little strange in this, but something strange is
    The unusual quickness of these common changes.
                       —Byron, *Don Juan*

Chapter One

"I shall marry the Earl of Carlington," Philippa Winslow suddenly remarked.

She sat in the cheerful east parlour at Wimcombe Manor behind a large tambour frame. The embroidered picture was all but finished; the glowing reds and yellows of its autumn flowers blended well with the polished woodwork and the bright fire in the room. Miss Winslow, however, was not looking at the work before her. She was gazing out the elegant French windows her grandfather had built in the old manor house. The view, that gloomy March evening, was not very pleasant. The trees were bare and the little brook at the foot of the park had chunks of ice floating in it. Their groom had predicted snow, and Miss Winslow was sure he was right. The grey clouds massed against the horizon looked threatening, and she shivered when she thought of the journey she was about to take.

Philippa was glad, after she had made her astounding pronouncement, to turn her head back to the room. Merely looking at its ruddy cherry-wood furniture, the engravings and watercolours that lined the walls, and the books heaped in a friendly fashion about the room made her feel happy and safe.

The only other occupant of the room was her brother, reading the latest *Edinburgh Review* with his feet comfortably propped on the firescreen. She expected an interesting response. She was disappointed. When Henry Francis realized the full import of her words, he showed no signs of his astonishment.

"Really, m'dear?" he inquired lazily. "Has he asked you?"

"Nooo," admitted Philippa, "but he will!"

"Most improbable."

"Not at all!" she retorted. "It would be different if I were setting out to catch his interest, but you can't deny that he has shown a great deal of interest in me already. He danced with me *three* times at Lady Jersey's ridotto, as well as taking me down to dinner."

"He talked the entire time about Lord Liverpool and the Privy Council, no doubt."

"I like having him speak to me of politics," Philippa said in a dignified tone. "No one else ever does."

"No one, Phil, but Lord Carlington pays any attention to the government."

"It's all the more worthy in him then. And I should like to be a Countess. And, when his father dies, a Marchioness!"

"A wealthy one!" said her brother with a bitter crack of laughter.

"Precisely," Philippa admitted. "Lord Carlington is handsome, cleverish, courteous, noble, and odiously well to let. And I know he likes me. With all that spurring me on, I should certainly be able to bring him up to scratch."

"Setting your sights just a bit too high," her brother replied calmly. "Think how uncomfortable such a *mésal-*

liance would be. Look at Cousin Adelaide, exiled in Bonn with her bounder of a husband for years. And I do hope you don't inform anyone else of your goal. Everyone's guessed, of course, but saying it aloud would make you look very foolish when you fail."

"You are not being very pleasant. You yourself told me of Father's debts, although goodness knows I should have known long ago, and you know as well as I that I must make a good marriage for the little ones' sake."

Wincing at his sister's bluntness, Henry Francis could not but agree: "It would be a splendid match, Phil, and solve all our problems, but don't depend on it. His father's in South America, of course, but if the Earl is truly considering you, his brother is just home from the Continent and is sure to do whatever he can to dissuade him from marrying a penniless girl."

"So you don't think I can do it! I can and I will marry Lord Carlington, and no one shall stand in my way," Philippa grandly declared.

"What about your friend the Spaniard instead? He's been very attentive."

"Too attentive for my taste. He's amusing, but forty if he's a day, Henry. And I couldn't move to Spain. Think how I'd miss Clarissa and Isabella and Robin!"

"And not me, I suppose?"

"Gudgeon," his sister said lovingly.

At this moment the butler entered the parlour, followed by a young lady with a basket over her arm.

"Miss Phelps," Holton announced as the Winslows rose to greet Henry Francis's *fiancée*.

Miss Phelps planted a kiss on Philippa's brow and accepted a chair next to Henry Francis. She removed her poke bonnet and carefully smoothed her pale blond hair.

"I have brought some calves-foot jelly for Clarissa," she explained. "I do hope she isn't seriously ill."

"I shouldn't think so, m'dear," Henry Francis said reassuringly. He rose to take Miss Phelps's basket and set it safely on the floor. "Philippa insists on returning to London today, but the note from Nanny merely said Clarissa had a fever."

"Henry Francis gives me too much credit," Philippa put in. "I was going back to London in a few days anyway."

"I shall miss you," Julia said, "but you must of course be with your sister. Do give her my love."

"I certainly shall. And you will have Henry Francis to bear you company."

"I shall make a point of riding over to the vicarage, every day, Julia," Henry Francis said.

Miss Phelps blushed. "I am sure you have many more important things to do," she protested.

"If he wishes to fritter away his time," Philippa smilingly told Julia, "I am sure he has a perfect right to do so. Don't you try to stop him!"

Julia gave a timorous giggle at this sally and Philippa went on.

"I shall drag him away from you soon enough. You promised you would come up for Lady Symington's ball, you know, Henry. It's the day after tomorrow. I shall be waiting for you!"

"I have every intention of escorting you as I promised, Philippa," her brother told her. "And I am looking forward to seeing the children again."

"How are the children?" Miss Phelps asked. "Do they miss Wimcombe?"

"Oh, yes." Philippa sighed. "*I* certainly do. But they enjoy the bustle of town life, and it is of course only for a time. When the season is over, we'll return to Oxfordshire."

"It will be pleasant having all of you back," Julia said. "You should come down more often."

"I won't deny this week has been most restful, but as long as I'm in London I think the children should stay. And I can't keep racketing back and forth. It might be amusing to leave the children with Henry, though—I hardly think he could handle them!"

"I thank you, my love," Henry Francis put in.

"She's quite right, Henry," Julia earnestly assured him. "You wouldn't like having them here at all."

"I admit it," he said, "but I do wish Philippa would stop living in London."

"What a shabby thing to say!" his betrothed exclaimed. "When you know how successful she is! All those *ton* parties and balls! Philippa's always mentioned in the *Gazette* as a 'star in the London firmament' and 'an accredited beauty'!"

"Julia, spare me!" Philippa moaned.

"It's true, and I think it's splendid. I clip all the notices about you."

"No, do you really?" Philippa asked with amusement. "I'm flattered, but pray don't believe a word, Julia!"

"But why not? You're just like the heroine of a novel," the vicar's fourth daughter, who had never had a London season, remarked ingenuously.

"Headstrong, impulsive, silly . . ." Henry Francis murmured.

"Thanks, love," Philippa said silkily. "Not but that you're right, I'm afraid. Closer to the truth than Julia, at any rate."

"But it's true, Philippa," her devoted friend assured her. "Everyone says so: Mama and Letty Barnes and Mrs. Kettering. Even Papa says you'll doubtless marry a duke or an earl, just like *Evelina*."

"She's trying to live up to your expectations," Henry Francis told Julia.

"Henry!" Philippa said in a minatory tone.

Her brother ignored her protest.

"I am surprised, Julia, that from the fashionable tit-tat you peruse you have not yet learned that Miss Philippa Winslow will shortly ensnare that rising young politician, that paragon of peers, the wealthy Earl of Carlington.

Elder son of the Marquis of Blawith—we'll see our Philippa a Marchioness before she dies."

Julia clasped her hands together. "Really, Philippa," she breathed. "How lovely!"

Philippa blushed. "Well, I don't know, Julia. I—I'd like to," she stammered.

"Oh," Julia said in disappointment. "But then why does Henry say—"

"I have faith in my sister, Julia," Henry Francis informed her. "Philippa has just decided, you see, to turn her mind to attaining this laudable goal. I am sure Lord Carlington will not stand a chance against her."

"Isn't," Julia murmured, "isn't that a little cold-hearted, Philippa? Or is Henry quizzing me?"

"Well, no," Philippa admitted. "I did say something of the sort a few minutes ago. But, er —it's the sensible thing, Julia!"

"To set your cap at the Earl? I suppose it is, but I'm disappointed in you."

"Oh, Julia," Philippa said in exasperation. "I know it's not romantic, but we need money. I must marry well! I don't see what's wrong in facing up to that."

"Yes you do, Phil, or you wouldn't be blushing now," her brother said.

"I'm not blushing!" Philippa furiously said. "You're to be a member of this family, Julia. You should know, if you don't already, just how hard it is to live with a spend-thrift father, and three children, and a position in society to keep up!"

"Philippa! You shouldn't speak like that of Sir Rupert. You must be very tired. A lady doesn't think of such things, at least not before she's married and takes on household responsibilities," she lamely ended.

"You're forgetting, Julia, that I've been *châtelaine* of this household since I was twelve. *I* shall marry a wealthy man and *forget* household responsibilities!" Philippa defiantly cried.

"Philippa, that will only lead to grief," Julia gently told her.

"Julia, you don't understand," Philippa said, calmer now. "I have always known it is up to me to marry well. I've been lucky and had a successful season—"

"More than successful—spectacular!" Julia loyally interposed.

"—and I've spent it looking for a man I can respect and who, quite frankly, can maintain my family. Women have to face that, Julia. My godmother was in the same position, my father's cousin Adelaide. So was her sister. No doubt her mother too."

"She married the Graf von Lansdorfer, didn't she?" Julia asked. "That wasn't a very happy marriage, by all reports."

"No, you're probably right, Julia. She wasn't very lucky. But she'd done her duty. And her sister, Helena's mother, married the Duke of Hetford! That was a happy marriage."

"While it lasted. Cousin Maria died three years later. And *our* mother didn't marry for money, Phil," Henry Francis drily said.

"If she had, dearest brother, then I wouldn't have to. But she married Father, who spends all the money he has or has ever had, and they had five children, and the consequence of that is that I should marry Lord Carlington if I possibly can."

"In my family, no one marries for money," Julia shyly put forward.

"Evidently, Julia—you're affianced to me!" Henry Francis retorted.

"The problem, Julia, is that my family has less money than yours—"

"Hardly, Philippa! Why, your father's a baronet!"

"An impoverished one, Julia. You know that. Just look at the grounds here. Wimcombe takes more money than we have," Henry Francis explained.

"—with, as I was saying," Philippa continued, "far greater pretensions and more expensive tastes. It would never have occurred to Father to economize by eliminating a London season for me or Harrow and Oxford for Henry Francis. We live above our station, Julia. Father will have a rude awakening when Robin *can't* go to Harrow and Isabella has to forego a *début*. That is, if I don't marry well."

"If you're sure of yourself, Philippa," Julia said dubiously, "maybe you'll be happy. But doesn't it seem cruel to your husband, expecting him to support your entire family?"

"Oh, not the entire family," Philippa airily answered. "You and Henry Francis can support yourselves here at Wimcombe, I daresay. But Carlington won't mind. That's why he's ideal. Fabulously wealthy—like his whole family —and willing to pay anything to avoid a bankruptcy and a scandal that would ruin his political chances. Just the son-in-law for Papa," she callously ended.

"But do you care for him, Philippa?" Julia asked in a serious tone. "Do you respect him? Could you spend the rest of your life with him?"

"Oh, if he's intolerable I can always retreat like the Duchess of York! I can breed dogs, just like her. Perhaps I should set up a canine cemetery at Pembley like the one at Oatlands!"

"Don't jest, Philippa," Julia pleaded. "The Duchess is married to a Prince Royal and her example is hardly to be emulated!"

"Marriage to one of the Princes is hardly conducive to happiness," Henry Francis darkly suggested.

"Quite, dear," Julia frankly agreed. "I don't think the Duchess is happy, shut away with her dogs, and, in any case, you're not an eccentric, Philippa!"

"No, merely odd and—what was your word, Henry? —headstrong!" Philippa said with a twinkle in her eye.

"Not really, Philippa. You must just be tired. I understand. Maybe you shouldn't go up to London this afternoon. Stay a few more days and rest, my dear," Julia advised.

"I'm fine, truly," Philippa said, rising lightly from her seat. "And Brownlow promised the coach would be ready to leave at three. I must see if Petherton has finished packing my things. Good-bye, Julia. It's been delightful seeing you. Take care of Henry Francis for me!"

"Philippa," Julia implored, "do think about this marriage. Wait a little. Perhaps you'll find someone as, as——"

"As truly admirable as your brother, Phil," Henry Francis finished.

"Well, yes," Julia shyly admitted, as Henry Francis put his hand over hers. "That is what I was going to say."

"But I never would find anyone comparable, Julia," Philippa sweetly retorted, her hand on the crystal doorknob. "I'm not as good as you are, or as credulous!"

With that Parthian shot, Miss Winslow withdrew, leaving her brother and Miss Phelps to a very enjoyable half-hour alone. At the end of it they emerged to wish Philippa a safe journey.

"Stop at 'The White Hart' in Watford for fresh horses, Brownlow," Henry Francis reminded the groom as he stowed three bandboxes safely aboard the antiquated coach. "You could go on to 'The Partridge' if necessary, but I think that would be pushing the horses. And don't let them bamboozle you at Watford! The change shouldn't take above fifteen minutes."

Brownlow, a placid and meek man, merely nodded at these orders, but Philippa summarily told her brother to be quiet.

"You're just delaying us, Henry, and I'm eager to be off. Clarissa's such a poor invalid. Thank you so much for the jelly, Julia. Petherton shall guard it in her lap all the way."

Philippa's elderly lady's maid unenthusiastically acquiesced in this arrangement, climbing into the forward seat with Brownlow's assistance and taking the glass jar carefully from the groom.

"Come up soon, Henry Francis," Philippa admonished her brother. "And don't listen to Julia. I am not tired at all. Why, I cannot wait to get back to London. There's Clarissa to be attended to, and I have other things to do."

"Indeed you do," Henry Francis said with meaning. "But don't try too hard. And have a safe journey."

Philippa took her pelisse and muff from him, kissed him and Julia, and climbed into the carriage. As it lumbered away from the manor, Philippa did feel tired for a moment. She leaned her head against the worn velvet panels of the old coach and waved good-bye to the calm old stone house nestled in the Chiltern hills. A visit to Wimcombe was always restful, she thought regretfully, and London life was always exhausting. But, brightening, she remembered ten-year-old Clarissa, who needed her, and she reflected that action, after all, could only be found in London. It was in London that she would find a husband, in London that her future would be decided. That thought was daunting at three in the morning or when talking to Julia Phelps, who was so infuriatingly passive and content, but most of the time Philippa found it invigorating. She was facing adventure, going back to the metropolis to carve her own destiny. Philippa closed her eyes and tried to sleep, hoping with all her heart that the tedious journey that delayed her plans would soon be over.

Chapter Two

Most people found the ride to London—almost four hours from Wimcombe—a dull one. Lord Charles Staunton certainly did. His carriage bowled smoothly along the well-maintained road. Lord Charles had no need to watch his driving; he was free to think about how good it was to be home.

He was but newly returned from Europe, having sold out of his regiment when Buonaparte was safely seen into exile for the second time. After the rigours of the Peninsular campaign and then—for he had not been home for five years—the war across Europe and the final rout at Waterloo, Lord Charles took pleasure in the comforts of English civilization: well-kept roads, plentiful cigars, home-brewed ale at the old inns that dotted the country-side—one of which, he knew, was just ahead. He had taken the reins from his coachman, and Lord Charles sang snatches of military songs as he peered ahead for "The White Hart." He was returning in a singularly good humour from a delightful visit with an old school friend. Thoroughly pleased with himself and the world, his only complaint, one for which he chided himself, was that civilian life grew dull.

His friend had happily settled on a country estate and recommended that Lord Charles do the same. Charles saw the appeal of establishing himself once again in the placid pattern of English life. The world in which he had been born and brought up was always the same. He had seen Buonaparte rock the very foundations of France, Spain, Portugal, Germany, Austria; only England remained unharmed. He had seen villages burned, churches gutted, women and children slain. He had dreamed, during all that, of the green pastures and crowded thoroughfares of his homeland, yet he was obscurely resentful when he returned and found his dreams borne out. England was idyllic, just as it had been in his childhood; that was the problem.

Lord Charles had suffered and matured during England's wars, while England had escaped unscathed. Many of Charles Staunton's friends were only too glad to rejoin proper society, as if the war had never happened, but he found it hard to forget the reckless courage he had painfully learned. The cheerful, indolent life he would have led without the war was alien to him now. It was not merely that he was hardened; he hoped he was not callous or bitter. He had simply grown accustomed to too rich a diet of heroism and adventure.

He had lived at a fever-pitch of excitement for many years, laughing in the face of danger, never relaxing, never sitting back and watching the rest of the world. That life hardly suited him for London's whirl of parties and scandals, tottering Governments, and shocking liaisons. The most serious intrigues and dramas of the *ton* seemed to him farcical. He only shrugged his shoulders, with a touch of wry amusement, at the Byron scandal that had all the town gossiping. He could not understand why people took these things so seriously. Charles Staunton had been endowed at birth with a light heart. War had not sobered him; it had just given him a sense of perspective that was rare in the upper reaches of London society. He was bored by the Prince Regent's latest exploits, thought Lady Jersey's juiciest *on-dits* intolerably dull, and found even his well-loved brother, with whom he was staying in town, longwinded and prosy. Lord Charles wished, as his perfectly matched greys whipped down the road to Watford, that something at least mildly interesting would happen.

His wish was to be almost immediately granted, in a quite dramatic form. As he whirled abruptly round a corner and—his mind at last on his driving—skidded precariously between two gateposts, coming to an elegantly-executed stop in the old innyard, Lord Charles saw the horridly familiar sight of smoke darkening the sky. He guessed, from the anguished neighs echoing through the yard, that a stable behind the inn was on fire. Several men were milling dazedly about the yard, appalled by the suddenness of this disaster. Wellington's scorched-earth policy had taught Charles Staunton much about fires, and he was both by birth and training accustomed to taking command. He leapt from his seat, curtly ordering his coachman to tether his horses at the far end of the yard, and addressed the nearest spectator, a pimply boy with a dazed look on his face.

"Is that the pump over there?" he demanded. "What are you standing about for? Run back to the kitchen. Fetch all the buckets there are. And anything else that will hold water. Hurry!"

Lord Charles quickly discarded his coat and greatcoat, wetted his handkerchief under the pump, and, clapping the linen square over his face, ran to the stable. He called for help and demanded of a portly, distressed man who seemed to have some authority if there were any people in the stable.

"No? Then for God's sake, get to the horses, man! All of you, quickly! Before it spreads!"

The dozen men in the cobbled yard were galvanized into action by Lord Charles's sudden commands. They dashed after him to bring the horses to safety and, once that was done, they threw buckets of water on the flames. Their efforts had little effect, however, and when another coach pulled into the yard some hours later, the stable, while it was no longer blazing, still smouldered dangerously. The village had been roused and many newcomers were filling and passing the heavy buckets. Lord Charles, with one arm nastily scorched, had finally been persuaded to take a break. He thirstily gulped down the mug of half-and-half the innkeeper's wife gave him and leaned against the high stone wall, breathing heavily and supporting himself with his good hand on the back of the old wooden bench picturesquely situated in the yard. It was he, grimy and sweaty though he was, who was accosted by the young lady whose carriage had just entered the yard, turning in from the far end.

Her coachman had evidently demurred at troubling this disreputable-looking young man, the only inhabitant of the innyard, but the intrepid young lady, in an elegant, cream-coloured pelisse, deftly clambered down from her coach, displaying for the admiring Lord Charles a neatly-turned ankle and quantities of lace-trimmed petticoat.

"You there," she called imperiously, "help me get a change of horses."

"What?" Lord Charles awfully demanded. "You want a change of horses?"

The lady, nettled by his tone, did not even notice his incongruously upper-class accent. "It's hardly an unreasonable request, my good man! I wrote ahead to procure them and it is your responsibility to have them ready for me. Have the goodness to get them immediately!"

She added, perhaps by way of excuse, "It truly is essential for me to get to London as soon as possible.

And my horses can go no further," but her general air was still decidedly arrogant and her statement was hardly palliative.

She almost stamped her foot as Lord Charles regarded her wonderingly, unmoving, slouched carelessly against the wall. "Can you understand me?" she said through her teeth. Miss Winslow's temper, never steady at the best of times, was shortened by her exhaustion and her worry about her sister.

Lord Charles, however, was also short-tempered, and now he finally moved. He covered the space between them in three quick strides and grasped Philippa by her shoulders.

"It may interest you to know, madam," he said, like Philippa through his teeth, "that the horses you so high-handedly demand have only narrowly escaped burning to death and this innkeeper, whom you fondly imagine to have been bustling about to obey your orders, has in fact been fighting a fire in the stable for the last three hours!"

Philippa idly thought that she had stupidly misjudged this man's class from his torn white shirt and grimy face, and then realized with a shock the import of his words. She turned to look behind her, beyond her coach, to the edge of the inn, where, from this angle, a score of busy people could be descried.

"They're fighting a fire over there?" she murmured contritely. "I'm sorry. I didn't know."

Lord Charles paid no attention to her apology. "The horses you want so badly are in no state, I can assure you, to be driven, and no one here has any time to spare for you. Sit there and don't speak!" he roughly ordered, pushing her to the wooden bench and, without looking back, he strode toward the stable.

Philippa was too mortified to protest. She collapsed meekly onto the bench, and sat there quietly, not daring even to tell Brownlow to take care of the horses. There was no need to, of course. Brownlow unharnessed and rubbed down the horses without a word from her. Then he went off to see what help he could render the fire-fighters, making Philippa feel even more guilty. She thought briefly of joining the crowd herself—there seemed to be a number of women and children aiding the men—but decided that, after having so grossly offended the unknown gentleman, the least she could do now was to obey his orders and hope for a chance to apologize properly.

She summed up her impression of the unknown gentleman as she sat there, hands decorously folded in her lap. He was tall, with a military walk. His thick hair was cut in an unremarkable Stanhope crop; his features were clear-cut, almost haughty. His coat of blue superfine, which, with the many-caped greatcoat, had been carefully folded by the innkeeper's wife and lain on the bench, was clearly made by Schulz, Philippa, trained by her father, noted with approval. He seemed altogether a prepossessing young man, despite their unlucky first encounter, and Philippa resolved to apologize very sweetly.

She had her chance soon enough. The fire seemed suddenly to decide it had spent itself. The smouldering beams sputtered and went out and, not half an hour after Miss Winslow had first driven into the innyard, the fire was over. Lord Charles, like everyone else there, was exhausted and ready to collapse. His arm ached badly and he was ravenously hungry. He barked an order to the ostler and walked round the inn to sluice his filthy head and arms under the pump in the yard. Shivering in the chill evening air, he walked wearily to the bench to retrieve his coats.

Philippa rose to greet him. She stood very still with her back to the wall. As he walked up, he didn't seem to notice her. She abruptly picked up his coats when he was still a few feet away and held them out to him.

"Here they are."

"Oh. Thank you."

Philippa felt foolish. She meant to apologize, but, face to face with this silent man, she found it hard to speak.

"Is the fire quite extinguished?"

"Yes." Lord Charles shrugged on his coat without looking at her. Turning to go, he appraised her with a cool glance from head to toe. "I'd hardly be here if it were still blazing, my dear," he drawled.

"You were here to greet me when—as you courteously informed me—the fire was still keeping most men busy!"

"I assure you, ma'am, I was not waiting to greet you."

"I deduced as much from the cordial reception you gave me," Philippa retorted.

"I shan't apologize to you for that, madam. You were damnably in the way!"

"I beg your pardon! This is a public inn, even if *one* of its patrons tries to dominate it! *You* are not the innkeeper, who, I hasten to remind you, makes his living by providing travellers with posthorses."

"A living and posthorses that I've just preserved for him!"

"And you say *I* am high-handed and arrogant!" Philippa cut in.

Lord Charles flushed.

The lady, seeing her advantage, pressed on. "I truly need to get to London as soon as possible! There's nothing unreasonable about that!"

Lord Charles had recovered his poise.

"Nothing in the world, madam. Indeed, to expedite your journey, I've sent a stableboy ahead to 'The Partridge' to obtain fresh horses. Your coachman's just reharnessing yours to drive there. You can be there in ten minutes—and the new team will be waiting for you." He bowed slightly and walked away.

Philippa stood still for a moment, torn between fury at

23

this unknown gentleman's high-handed managing of her affairs and gratitude for the trouble he had taken. The latter emotion won out and she ran across the yard after him. He was about to enter the inn, his hand on the oaken door, but turned at the sound of her footsteps.

"I—I'm so sorry!" Philippa said breathlessly. She smiled up at him. "Thank you so much. I've been behaving abominably."

Lord Charles laughed. He looked down at Philippa's ingenuous face under her modish bonnet of celestial blue.

"No, don't feel guilty," he told her. "Don't think about it at all."

Then, as much to his surprise as Philippa's, he put his arm around her and kissed her swiftly and expertly.

None of the most disreputable of the young bucks who admired Philippa had ever dared touch her thus, and, though she struggled against him, for one moment she felt a crazy urge to respond. But Lord Charles set her free abruptly. He bowed slightly.

"May I wish you a safe journey? Perhaps we shall meet in London."

Philippa, wide-eyed, could only murmur, "An unlikely possibility."

"And unwelcome too, I've no doubt," Lord Charles chuckled. He flicked her cheek lightly with one finger. "But we shall see. Good day, ma'am."

He bowed slightly once again and retired to the inn.

Philippa turned to face her coach where Brownlow, indeed, was harnessing up the horses. He had seen nothing of her *rencontre* with the dark young man who knew just what to do in case of fire and for whom he had conceived an immense admiration. Petherton, Philippa's easily shocked abigail, had fortunately been dozing in the coach all this while, and Philippa clambered up and drove off without having to say a word about the astonishing incident.

Petherton slept through the change of horses at "The

Partridge" and most of the way to London, but Philippa did not mind the lack of company. As before, she was occupied with her own thoughts, resting her chin on her hand and gazing dreamily out the window. She had stopped thinking, however, of Clarissa and the admirable Earl of Carlington; a dark, clear-cut face with a mocking smile kept reappearing before her.

Chapter Three

Miss Winslow arrived at her father's elegant Georgian house in Half Moon Street some hours later that evening. Leaving Petherton to deal with the unpacking, she ran lightly up the stairs, hardly pausing to discard her pelisse and muff before seeing little Clarissa. Philippa didn't leave Clarissa's bedside for some time. Clarissa, though on the high road to recovery, was a fussy girl and insisted her beloved elder sister sit beside her while she tried to sleep. Philippa's brothers and sisters had seen little of her this year. As a toast of the town, she was always running off to a masquerade or a ridotto, never failing to show off her gown and to kiss each of the little ones (Philippa and Henry Francis thought even of fifteen-year-old Isabella that way, much as she rebelled against the description) before she left for the evening. They missed her, nevertheless, in the nursery where she had formerly spent much of her time. Clarissa thus clung to this chance to have

Philippa's undivided attention. When she finally relaxed and slept, Philippa tiptoed out of the room and collapsed in her own bed. It was not until the morning of the next day was considerably advanced that she came downstairs after breakfast in her room and greeted her father.

He was standing in the elegant (although the damask curtains were, as Philippa well knew, fading badly) drawing-room, tossing dice from one hand to the other. Sir Rupert Winslow was still a handsome man, and a charming one, but now his brightly-coloured waistcoats bulged alarmingly and his cravat was less tidily arranged than had been his wont in his youth. He had given up his youthful pretensions to dandyhood, and he had faintly seedy air of a self-indulgent man.

Philippa entered quickly, Jarvis, the butler, having informed her of her parent's whereabouts, and pulled two of the fashionable Sheraton chairs to face each other.

"Father," she peremptorily said, "I must talk to you."

"Damme, Philippa, it's half-past one already and I'm due at Cripplegate's at two."

"I don't like Lord Barrymore," Philippa said decidedly, having been the victim of Lord Barrymore's unpleasant attentions more than once. "I must speak with you, and *you* must sit down at once and listen to me."

"Very well, what is it?" Sir Rupert impatiently demanded.

Philippa, plunging into the problem, bravely answered. "We need to hire another housemaid. This house is too big to be handled by a staff of six. Especially if— as we must—we do any entertaining in the next few months."

"Very well, then, Philippa. Hire a housemaid."

"But Father, I don't want to unless we can afford to pay her!" Philippa expostulated. "Can we?"

"How should I know, my girl? I don't keep account of all our money!"

"Yes, Father," Philippa said sharply. "I am very, very well aware of that!"

Sir Rupert had the grace to blush. He had always lived extravagantly—Philippa dimly recalled her usually placid mother bursting into tears as yet another bailiff demanded entrance—but since Lady Winslow's death seven years before he had imperceptibly moved into the disreputable circle of Hell-Fire boys surrounding the lame Lord Barrymore, known as "Cripplegate," and his equally repellant brothers, "Hellgate" and "Newgate." Sir Rupert was on intimate terms with the Cyprians and pugilists who frequented Daffy's Club, and he was in great demand at every cockfight and sparring-match held in London. His manners were, when outside the bosom of his family, impeccable, and he was exceedingly open-handed with his money, whether to one of the Fashionable Impures or to his tailor. He was everywhere acknowledged and acclaimed as a good-natured, jovial chap, and he was very proud of this reputation. Sir Rupert could not be brought to see, as Philippa often said despairingly to her brother, that even the mildest profligacy accorded ill with the demands of a moderate income and a large family. Henry Francis, with all the weight of his twenty-six years, austerely declared that their father's conduct would perhaps have been excusable in his salad days, but that there was no sight more unpleasant than that of a middle-aged *débauché*. To be sure, he did not use quite those words when speaking to his younger sister, but her vivid imagination credited her father, fond as she was of him, with crimes all the more heinous for being unspoken.

Henry Francis resembled his mother, quiet and phlegmatic, with the strength of his convictions. He was content to be a country squire and a good one. He was a Justice of the Peace, took good care of his father's tenants, and took his responsibilities with his younger sisters and brother very seriously. He strongly disapproved of his father and was suspicious of London society altogether. At twenty-six, he looked thirty.

Philippa, no less than her brother, disapproved of her father's manner of living, but she could do little about it. She had brought up the children since her mother's death when she was twelve, and she was responsible beyond her years. However, this London season, where brunettes were in and she had been such an astonishing success, had proved seductive. She, far more than Henry Francis, could understand her father's frivolity. For one accustomed since early girlhood to household chores and domestic troubles, to dance till three seemed indeed high heaven. She was *aux anges* when a Royal Duke paid her a compliment or when she received a flattering invitation. Her joy at such trivialities always made her realize sharply that she might be more like her father than she knew, to care so much for society's fripperies. Her resentment of her father's behaviour increased, unfairly, as she herself participated to some extent in the life he led with such gusto. She remained aloof and condemnatory, making Sir Rupert, who was very fond of her, unhappy.

He was always soon consoled, though, as Philippa well knew. Her concern about her father in the last few months had been as much to keep him from shocking the eminently respectable Earl of Carlington by some impolite statement as to have him refrain from coming home in the small hours, carolling loudly down Half Moon Street, or, which was worse, gambling all night. Sir Rupert, strangely enough, although he had lately been winning considerable sums, never seemed to profit from his games.

Philippa was just pointing this out to her father in the drawing-room, since he had just offered, if his luck was in that night, to pay for a new housemaid from his winnings at cards.

"Damme, m'girl, didn't I give your £10 for household expenses just last week?"

"Yes, and it was very welcome, but your winnings at

the card table are not to be relied on, Father, as a source of income! You always end up losing far more than you win, and we can't afford it! If this goes on, this house will have to be sold, and we'll all have to retire to Wimcombe. You'll have to sell out of the Funds, and God only knows what would become of us. You must stop, Father!"

"Philippa, you are not to speak to me like that," her father blustered. "Things have come to a pretty pass if a little snip of a girl can be standin' up to her own father, bold as brass, tellin' him what he 'must' do. I'd not have thought it of you, Philippa, and I'll have no more 'musts' from you or any other of my children!"

"Father," Philippa said, striving for a reasonable tone, "I would like you to circumscribe your behaviour for at least the rest of this season. It's really most dreadfully important that you behave yourself!"

"What have you got up your sleeve, my girl?"

"Frankly, Papa, I think I must marry."

"Marry money, eh? Who do you have in mind? Lord Carlington? Or that pompous windbag of an Iberian? Carlington's the better match, you know. Marquis of Blawith's heir. And all that family has money. Grandfather was an Indian nabob, I believe. Though I'd be a bit dubious about marrying Blawith's son. They say the old man has gone absolutely mad. He's been watching birds in Brazil for years."

"Lord Carlington isn't like that at all. He's a very sober young man. He's very highly thought of in Parliament," Philippa said stiffly.

"Yes, but do you want to marry him? Dash it all, Philippa, he's a dull dog. Worthy, I don't say he ain't worthy, but dull!"

"He's very respectable, very proper. He has the highest standards of conduct. I do want you to behave yourself."

"Philippa, you don't seriously think you can pull

this off, do you? Carlington must be one of the most eligible men in England!"

"I do think I can pull it off, Father, in your rather unpleasant phrase. He admires me—and I like him. But I am worried about making a wrong impression. Please, Father dear, please behave yourself."

"Don't worry, my girl. It'd be a dashed good thing if you could catch the Earl. I shan't queer your game. I'll keep out of your way."

"Thank you, Father. You do see how important it is?"

"Oh, yes. I know how little money we have! It's been a bad year, Philippa. A bad year!"

"I thought you just said you *didn't* know how much money we have."

"I know enough about it, my dear, to know we're in trouble. And that's as much as you know, or as much as you ought to," Sir Rupert said severely. "You should be ashamed of yourself, countin' pennies for a servant's wages like a Cit! Talking about entrappin' a husband! Go and do it, but it's dashed *bourgeois* to talk about it!"

"Yes, Papa," Philippa said meekly. "I shall try, sir, to cultivate your more refined and insouciant attitude."

Sir Rupert cast a suspicious glance at his favourite daughter. "Oh, get along with you! I suppose someone has to count pennies! Just wish it weren't my daughter. You're too pretty to bother your head with finances."

"I feel that way often enough, Father," Philippa assured him. "That's why I shall marry the fabulously wealthy Earl and live in opulence forever more. *If* you don't scare him off!"

"I'll be as good as—as good as Henry Francis," her father promised.

Philippa smiled. "Then I have nothing to fear."

She embraced her erratic but endearing father and ran upstairs to collect Isabella and Robin for the walk she had promised them in the Green Park.

Chapter Four

It was a bright and clear day, and the Park was filled with promenaders. Robin played tag with another little boy, and Isabella, though she was really too old for it, chased her hoop, while Philippa, despite her shabby walking-dress, was greeted by many of her elegant acquaintances. They had a lovely two hours in which Philippa almost forgot her ambition. It was brought back to her mind as soon as they entered the house, a few minutes before the children's nuncheon was scheduled.

"Lord Carlington has been awaiting your return in the morning-room, Miss Philippa," Jarvis informed her.

Philippa quickly entered the morning-room without stopping to take off her bonnet. She spoke cordially as she closed the door behind her and stepped forward to meet him.

"Good afternoon, Lord Carlington. How are you to-day?"

"Very well, thank you, Miss Winslow. May I say that

I don't need to inquire as to your health? You look charming."

Philippa, amused by his heavy-handed compliment, murmured a quiet thank-you.

"I have come to ask if you will join me in a ride round the Park, Miss Winslow."

Philippa laughed and explained that she had just returned from a stroll there.

"But I was with the children, which hampered conversation. I assure you, no sooner had I greeted Lady Sefton than I had to run to Robin's rescue! He had met a large mongrel that must have followed him for half a mile! We had great trouble brushing the dog off; I verily believe it wanted to adopt us! I should be absolutely delighted to spend a quiet time in the park. I can rely on you, this time, to repel any unwanted animals."

Lord Carlington smiled at her chatter and expressed his pleasure at her assent.

Isabella and Robin were peering out of the well-barred nursery window on the third floor at Lord Carlington's handsome bays as their sister emerged. She had changed into a dashing green riding-habit of which she was particularly fond. The children admired it from their vantage point, but Robin said he didn't like Lord Carlington.

"You've never met him, silly," answered his elder sister.

"I mean I don't like the looks of him," Master Winslow replied haughtily.

"Why not?" asked Isabella, momentarily intrigued. "Does he look wicked, Robin?" Isabella pushed her brother aside eagerly. She was disappointed. Carlington was no brooding Byronic hero, but a heavy-set blond man, with a smiling, round countenance and a slow, deliberate air.

"I don't like him either," Isabella said. "He looks dull. Not Phil's sort."

Robin agreed heartily, but Philippa, happily unaware of their strictures, was actually enjoying her ride very much. Henry Francis would see that she could marry an Earl, and would! She smiled sweetly at Lord Carlington, and, to make him happy, inquired about matters at Westminster.

"Parliament is functioning much as usual, Miss Winslow. Lord Castlereagh made a brilliant speech in the Lords yesterday on the Government's new agreement with Austria. I am myself preparing a reply."

"How exciting," Philippa breathed. Lord Carlington was one of the most important young men in the Whig Opposition, as she, and he, knew well, but to be assigned to make the reply to the Foreign Secretary's latest speech was an unexpected honour. "How pleased you must be!"

"Indeed, Miss Winslow, my pleasure is not unmixed with timorousness. I have, of course, spoken before on issues of significance in the House, but to reply to the Viscount's speech on a subject of such paramount importance could daunt, truly, a Pitt or a Fox!"

"Yes, of course," Philippa contented herself with answering.

Lord Carlington was only too happy with even this slight encouragement to continue.

"Lord Castlereagh is a man of unquestioned integrity and ability, as I am sure you are aware, Miss Winslow, but his political views are unalterably opposed to my own."

"Yes, I understand." Philippa and her family had been Whigs for generations—even her otherwise disreputable father subscribed to the *Edinburgh Review*—and she sourly thought that that was fortunate indeed; Lord Carlington would never marry into a Tory family. In that she did him an injustice. Lord Carlington was not a demanding man, and to have lovely Philippa Winslow ready to listen to his tales of Parliamentary doings was quite enough for him to think of her as a suitable wife. It would not have mattered to him had her father and grandfather been Tories of the deepest dye; she, he assumed, would naturally agree with her husband on any question. He was very sure Miss Winslow would do so, and she was so devoted and so charming that he had almost made up his mind to offer for her. He had spoken to his brother and his mother about it, and they had approved.

"Carlington," his mother remarked to his younger brother, "is made for dull domesticity," and everyone who knew him, including Philippa Winslow, could not but agree. Of course, Miss Winslow was not the ideal wife for him, as she was of genteel rather than noble birth, and her fortune was known to be small, but she was a reigning beauty, and a singularly well-mannered, if eccentric, young lady. The Marchioness of Blawith had been pleased with the idea of Carlington's marriage, although she afterward expressed some doubts to her younger son (who took after her rather than his father), that Miss Winslow was really too lively for the Earl. The Marchioness, an elegant bluestocking, knew to what trouble that could lead. Carlington was precisely like his father; where his ruling passion was politics, the Marquis of Blawith's was birds. Lord Blawith was an ardent ornithologist and had spent the last four years in South America, observing birds. Lady Blawith had gone out there with him, but, as she had no interest at all in his hobby, she had returned to England without her husband. She heard from him once or twice a year. Theirs had been a placid separation, but the marriage could hardly be called successful. Lady Blawith liked Philippa, whom she had met on one of the rare occasions on which she ventured into society, but, although she never said so, even to her younger son, the Marchioness was convinced Philippa Winslow was too clever for her son.

Philippa might, at that moment, have agreed. They had been riding for a half-hour and had spoken of nothing but Prince Metternich, the deplorable state of the Austrian monarchy, and Lord Carlington's projected speech. Philippa was heartily bored, and when she saw an acquaintance approaching, was delighted to be able to interrupt Lord Carlington and ask him to stop.

"Don Fernando,' she called. "How delightful to see you!"

Don Fernando de Santiago y Anandas's rubicund face brightened at this encouraging greeting from the lady whom he had thought indifferent to his heart-felt advances.

"But you, dear lady, have more than delighted, you have overwhelmed me. What more pleasure can a man have than to see a goddess on a heavenly morning such as this?"

Philippa, unlike most young ladies of her time, did not place much credence in this or the other protestations of love and admiration with which Don Fernando had favoured her. She was slightly embarrassed, but amused, and became more amused when she saw Lord Carlington's expression of disgust.

You two have not met, I believe," she said, as the two carriages drew closer to each other. "Lord Carlington, may I present Don Fernando de Santiago y Anandas? Don Fernando is here on a special visit with the Ambassador to study English trade. Don Fernando, the Earl of Carlington."

"How do you do? Are you a merchant, then, Don Fernando?" Lord Carlington asked with only the slightest hint of condescencion in his well-bred voice.

"Yes, indeed," replied the Spaniard. "I've been quite successful lately with the exportation of coffee and spices." He continued to expound on his business for several minutes.

Philippa reflected that, although Lord Carlington was quite as boring as Don Fernando, the Earl was unable to bear another's harangues. He was far too courteous to interrupt the Spaniard, but as he sat there, entwining his fingers in the reins, tapping his foot, and looking stormy, Philippa was hard put not to laugh. Don Fernando, who was not at all stupid, saw the nobleman's discomfort and Philippa's lack of attention (far sooner, indeed, than Carlington would have) and begged pardon.

"I fear I have been running on. Miss Winslow looks tired. Ah, one cannot expect lovely ladies to interest themselves in business matters."

Philippa thought with exasperation that she almost preferred Carlington's manner. He spoke at greater length, but he at least allowed that she was fully capable of understanding what he was saying. But Don Fernando was still speaking.

"Shall I see you at Lady Symington's ball tomorrow night, Miss Winslow?"

"Yes, of course." Philippa smiled. "Her parties are always so splendid!"

"Where the flowers ever blossom, the beams ever shine/Where the light wings of Zephyr, oppress'd with perfume/Wax faint o'er the gardens of Gûl in her bloom."

Philippa knew of Don Fernando's fervent admiration for the verses of Lord Byron, but Lord Carlington, who did not, was considerably bewildered by the Spaniard's outburst and Philippa's indulgent smile.

"Precisely, Don Fernando," Philippa said. "It will be a true crush, with the best food and music in town. Everybody will be there."

"Then I assume I shall see you too, Lord Carlington, at Lady Symington's ball?"

"Er, yes, yes, of course," stammered Carlington as he understood the question. He had received a card, but he had not planned to attend. However, if Philippa were going, he wouldn't miss it.

"Will you waltz with me, Miss Winslow?" the Earl asked.

"The very first one!" Philippa cordially replied. A

public waltz with a young lady was a declaration of definite interest, she exultantly told herself, and the first waltz of an evening was always the most important. The Earl was thinking that this ball would be an excellent opportunity to introduce Philippa to his newly-returned brother, whom he hoped would like his intended bride.

Philippa would have been a good deal happier had she known that Lord Carlington so styled her in his own mind. Her future would then be comfortably settled and she would be able to fend off importunate suitors. True, she had not too many suitors to deal with; she was much admired, but her lack of fortune, as she knew, meant that those admirers who actually came up to snuff and offered for her were almost always quite ineligible. It made her good luck in attracting the interest of the Earl of Carlington all the more remarkable. He could, it was true, marry where he wished, but rich men, the *ton* had long ago noticed, tended to choose equally well-endowed wives. Philippa knew how unlikely her chances of success with Lord Carlington were, and, despite her confident declaration to her brother, she was very careful not to lose her only other serious and wealthy admirer, Don Fernando. It was imperative that she wed a rich man, and thus she could not afford to cast off even the dullest one. She smiled sweetly at Don Fernando each time they met, but she dreamed of the day she could simply ignore him. Not that she disliked Don Fernando, far from it, she found him one of the pleasanter unmarried men in London, but she did dislike being obliged to listen to his fulsome compliments and to pretend she liked them.

If only Carlington would come up to snuff, Philippa thought, everything would be wonderful! Lost in a beatific dream of herself as the Countess of Carlington, or, if his father died, the Marchioness of Blawith, giving delightful little political parties to the friends of her husband, who was spoken of as the next Prime Minister, if Liverpool and the Duke of Wellington were eliminated at one stroke, Philippa didn't think about her boredom with political affairs, and, indeed, her boredom with fashionable life. Philippa had spent all her life among the *ton*. Even during her childhood in Wimcombe, she had led a dashing life as Sir Rupert Winslow's eldest daughter. She had had enough of it, although she didn't realize it yet; she needed adventure, a change, a breath of fresh air, which she was singularly unlikely to get with Lord Carlington. Before her common-sense made her face this fact, however, they had reached Half Moon Street. Philippa, thanking Lord Carlington prettily, alighted and went inside to minister to her afflicted sister.

Chapter Five

At eleven o'clock the next morning Miss Winslow could be seen entering Hookham's Lending Library on Bond Street. It was a lovely, crisp morning, with a hint of the coming spring in the warm breeze that rustled the leaves on the trees and sadly disarranged Philippa's elegant *Sappho* hairstyle. The sun shone brightly, and the fashionable shopping streets were filled with ladies in primrose or pink gowns and gentlemen attired in similar springlike shades. Philippa was wearing a pink sarcenet frock, an old one that she would never wear to a formal occasion, but of which she was very fond. The rose-colored ribbons on her straw bonnet completed the outfit, and not one in ten of the many people who saw her walk, her reticule and parasol over her arm, down the street would have noticed that her dress was the year before last's style and that her ribbons had been dyed to match it.

Philippa had refused any escort for her morning's

excursion. It was the day of Lady Symington's ball, and Philippa wanted some exercise in the open air before the party. She was not, despite her gay chatter to Don Fernando looking forward to five hours spent in an overcrowded room with the same dull people she saw every day. She would drink too much champagne, dance with young men who had drunk even more than she, laugh the laugh that the Prince Regent himself called "silvery," and talk with Lord Carlington about politics and Don Fernando about spices. The prospect would usually have pleased her, and Philippa idly wondered if she were ill. The leaders of society were, it was understood, supposed to be bored with everything they did, but a young lady in only her second season (however sophisticated and wordly-wise Philippa might feel herself to be) was supposed to be in an ecstatic trance; Philippa knew that much of her charm and appeal lay in her naïveté, her clear delight in things her elders, like Lord Carlington or even Henry Francis, had learned to scorn. It had been kind of Henry Francis to agree to return in time for Lady Symington's ball, Philippa admitted. He wouldn't enjoy it, she knew, but Sir Rupert would not conceivably attend, and Philippa wanted badly to have a member of her family at the ball to lend her countenance. At Almack's last week, Princess Esterhazy had commented on her family's absence; it would be too embarrassing to have neither her brother nor her father at Lady Symington's ball as well.

So Philippa strode down Bond Street at a brisk pace, ignoring the ogles of the *demi-beaux* and the cries of the peddlars on all sides of her. She waved to several of her acquaintances who drove by in their phaetons, but laughingly refused all offers of a lift. Such behaviour would be strongly censured in any other young lady—venturing forth unattended was daring indeed—but Philippa Winslow had long ago been recognized as as much an original as she was a beauty, and society allowed her to do very much as she wished.

Society, of course, Philippa reflected as she walked along, did not know her destination. She suppressed a desire to glance furtively about to see if anyone were watching her as she marched up the marble steps leading to Hookham's, London's literary emporium. While most young ladies read novels, and *romans à clef* were immensely popular, it was still frowned upon for such a very young lady as Miss Winslow, who was already compromised by owning such a disreputable (if charming) father, to be seen reading the lurid romances that filled the library's shelves. Philippa had not even come for herself as much as for Isabella, who read these stories with a passionate interest, and in hopes that she could find something suitable for little Clarissa. Clarissa, never an easy child, had balked on being told that she must stay in bed for at least the rest of the week. Phillippa had placated her only by promising to bring her something exciting to read to occupy her time. Henry Francis, who did not really approve of novel-reading, particularly not in a girl of Clarissa's age, had long since agreed with Philippa that, in times of illness, it was cruel to leave a child with only *The Pilgrim's Progress, The History of the Good Child,* or the collected sermons of some long-dead divine to beguile her hours. Accordingly, Philippa boldly plunged into the library to honour her little sister's request.

As Philippa scanned the shelves to see what new romances had been published, she was greeted by a dear friend.

"Philippa, my dear! So you have returned to London," Lady Helena Prescott said.

"Cousin Helena! What *are* you doing here? You don't approve of novels!"

Lady Helena, a tall, short-sighted woman with pale brown hair and a quiet manner, smiled.

"The Princess Esterhazy begged me to accompany her, my dear."

"I see," Philippa nodded. "Here's the Princess now."

The Princess Esterhazy, *soignée* as always, lowered a cool cheek for Philippa to kiss.

"Ah, my dear Miss Winslow, I am glad to see you have rejoined us in the metropolis," the wife of the Austrian ambassador pronounced. "You will attend Aurelia Symington's ball tonight?"

"Yes, of course," Philippa answered.

"And your so-charming parent?"

"I can't really say, madam."

"Your brother, then?"

Philippa, hoping desperately that he wouldn't fail her, responded promptly. "I believe so."

"Good." The Princess smiled. "And now I must leave. But don't, *ma chère Hélène,* desert your cousin, I beg you. You two will have things to talk of. I shall see you both tonight. Good day."

The Princess sailed majestically away, her footman bearing the books she had selected, and Philippa, somewhat relieved, hugged Helena impulsively.

"I am so glad to see you, *chérie,*" she said. "You know Clarissa's ill?"

"No, I did not," Helena replied. "I am sorry to hear it. A fever?"

"Yes—but I'm not worrying unduly. I came back up from Wimcombe as soon as I heard, but she seems already to be on the high road to recovery."

"You must be considerably relieved."

"Yes indeed," Philippa answered. "I knew she was well when she sat up and demanded something unedifying and improper to read!"

"Don't jest, Philippa. You are surely not going to give the child *Thaddeus of Warsaw?*" Lady Helena reprovingly asked as she glanced at the marble-covered novel Philippa had just plucked from the shelf.

"No, this is for me," Philippa airily said. "But I shall get her a novel, Helena—I don't think one will corrupt her. And I was prepared for far more arduous duties! I spent the journey to London worrying about hiring nurses."

This was not strictly true, but Lady Helena was always inclined to believe the best of her acquaintances. "You poor child! I hope the ride wasn't too fatiguing. When did you return? Yesterday?"

Philippa nodded and, although aware that Lady Helena's Evangelical principles made her a far from ideal confidante, decided to tell her of her adventure.

"And the most curious incident occurred, Helena!"

She launched into an explanation. Lady Helena quite impartially condemned both her cousin and the unknown young man's behaviour, until Philippa blushingly finished her story: "And then, then he *kissed* me, Helena!"

"Philippa!" her scandalized auditor ejaculated. "What a shameful thing! In a public innyard! You must have encouraged him in some way!"

"I swear I didn't," Philippa indignantly hissed in an undertone, as she saw that several people, fortunately strangers, had heard Lady Helena's statement.

"You must learn to restrain your natural friendliness, Philippa. It is most unbecoming. You shouldn't have spoken to the young man at all. Far worse could have happened."

Philippa shuddered and, regretting already her confidence, meekly listened to a long stricture on her careless manners. She diverted her cousin, finally, by enlisting her aid in selecting books for Clarissa, whom she basely betrayed, taking for her, on Lady Helena's recommendation, Mrs. More's excellent moral tale—for it could not be sullied with the name of novel—*Coelebs in Search of a Wife.*

Some half-hour later the ladies descended the elegant marble steps down to Bond Street, Philippa laden—for her own consumption, she firmly told Lady Helena—with an armload of the most lurid tales Mr. Hookham could procure for her. It was noon by now, and the street was crowded with people of all descriptions. Philippa swerved to avoid a particularly formidable matron bearing down on her, and tripped.

It was all very well and romantic to trip if a gentleman were at hand to catch one, but extremely embarrassing when alone on a street filled with *demi-beaux* and the London poor. In preserving her dignity she lost her burden—the books tumbled from her arms and scattered. Philippa laughed and, ignoring the cat-calls of the young men across the street, proceeded to gather the volumes up as quickly as she could. Lady Helena, embarrassed, could not come to Philippa's assistance, laden as she was with a new life, in four volumes, of the Electress Sophia.

Philippa had not realized that there was indeed more than one gentleman at hand who would have been only too happy to help her had she fallen. She raised her head, smiling triumphantly at having recovered all of her books, only to see her mysterious gentleman of the innyard and the Earl of Carlington. They were regarding her with, respectively, amusement and pity, and the unknown gentleman immediately stepped forward and bowed.

"Miss Winslow, I believe? I am so glad to have the pleasure of meeting you."

Philippa thought fleetingly that at least he had not added 'again" and, as he deftly removed the books from her arm, mutely turned to Lord Carlington for an explanation.

"Miss Winslow, may I present my brother Charles, of whom you have heard me speak so often? How fortunate we are to meet you here!"

Philippa did not agree. Her senses reeled; this was surely the most awkward situation in which she had ever found herself. Lady Helena, who knew the Earl and his brother well, was perfectly at ease, and Lord Charles had taken Philippa's appearance in stride, with a smile and a quizzically raised eyebrow. Philippa, however, was blushing furiously, and she was acutely aware, as she had not been even with the Princess Esterhazy, of her shabby frock.

"How do you do, Lord Charles?" she asked politely, swallowing her astonishment. Without waiting for an answer she started telling Lord Carlington, whom she could see noticed nothing amiss, about the excellent new biography of the King's unhappy ancestress that Lady Helena had procured. She had spoken for fully a minute before she realized Lord Charles was speaking.

"I'm very happy to be in England again," he said, apparently in answer to her earlier question. "So peaceful and unravaged. Nothing much ever seems to happen here. The biggest disaster since Culloden is doubtless a burning stable."

Philippa lifted her chin defiantly. If he could do this, so could she. She, after all, had done nothing to be ashamed of.

"Have you ever seen a burning stable, Lord Charles?" she ingenuously inquired.

"I'm sure he's seen hundreds," Lady Helena, who had just been assailed by a horrid suspicion, replied. "Lord Charles was in Spain, you know, Philippa."

Lord Carlington, happily unaware of any undertones to this conversation, proudly said, "He even saw one the day before yesterday, driving to London. He put it out, of course. Rotten sort of welcome in one's first week, I think."

"Yes, indeed," said Philippa. "I can imagine few things more disconcerting than driving into an innyard and seeing a stable on fire!"

Lord Carlington laughed heartily. "Particularly if you expect to get a change of horses!"

47

"We must hope," Lord Charles smoothly said, "that Miss Winslow is never troubled with such an unpleasant scene."

Lady Helena, whose suspicion had been confirmed, stared at Lord Charles with undisguised horror. Philippa blushed. Just then Lord Carlington realized the impropriety of standing in the middle of the street and asked Miss Winslow and Lady Helena if he and his brother might have the honor of escorting them home.

"Yes, of course." Philippa flashed him one of her sweetest smiles. This girl is too clever by half for Carlington, Lord Charles thought to himself.

As they strolled down the street toward Lord Carlington's phaeton, from which the gentlemen had emerged for a visit to Sturges' Bank, Charles looked at the books he was holding.

"Are you always so sentimental?" he asked Miss Winslow as he helped her up, while his brother directed the coachman. Philippa blushed for the third time in minutes at being caught with an armload of novels. Lord Carlington, she knew well, would not approve. Firmly taking the books back as she settled into the comfortable seat, she laughed and said:

"Not at all; I'm very hard-headed."

"I can see that," Lord Charles replied, glancing at his oblivious brother.

Philippa inwardly smiled. If she could convince Lord Charles that she was a fortune-hunter, then although he might try to stop her betrothal, he would not at least continue flirting with her. Her open hostility would be very unpleasant—it might, indeed, spoil all her plans—but it was far better than over-amorousness.

Charles, however, was far from convinced. She was clever, that was clear, and she obviously intended to marry his brother. He had thought, when his brother told him of his *tendre* for a witty and lively young beauty, that the attachment sounded disastrous. A man of Carling-

ton's sober mien and practical outlook on life would surely regret being tied to a social butterfly, and one who
sounded considerably cleverer than the Earl. On meeting
her, and recognizing her, he began to think again. Truly,
she was very different from Carlington, but when around
her Carlington (although Philippa would never have believed it) was far less dull than usual. Philippa Winslow
brought to Carlington a certain gaiety, a *joie de vivre* that
he sadly lacked. It might not work, but Lord Charles
decided he liked the girl. He liked girls with spirit, and
he'd a thousand times rather have her for his sister-in-
law, even if she was penniless and eccentric, than one of
the Friday-faced spinsters his brother usually turned to.
Besides, Philippa Winslow was damned amusing to talk
to, knowing what he did.

"And did you suffer from any unpleasantness in
your journey, Miss Winslow?" he solicitously asked.

Lady Helena, who had always thought Charles
Staunton a very nicely mannered young man, could only
gasp dumbfounded.

Philippa managed not to blush this time, and replied
coolly: "Yes, but I arrived home unaffected by any of
the hardships of my journey."

Touché, thought Lord Charles. "One must hope,
Miss Winslow, that those hardships were not many."

"No, merely decidedly distasteful."

Now it was Lord Charles's turn to blush.

"What hardships?" Lord Carlington asked. "You
were all right, weren't you? The ride from Wimcombe
didn't tire you, surely?"

"Of course not," Philippa smiled. "It was not so
ungentlemanly as to trouble me unduly."

Charles suppressed a laugh; Lady Helena darted
an admonitory glance at her young cousin.

"I am glad to hear it," Carlington said.

Lady Helena felt it was time to change the subject.
"Your mother always says, Carlington, that women are

too gently bred nowadays. Her generation would regard a jaunt to Edinburgh as nothing."

"Admirable," Lord Charles exclaimed. "Mother is quite right. There's too much coddling today."

"Surely you don't want women to suffer, Charles?" his brother asked.

"A little jostling over rough roads could only do them good," Lord Charles callously said. "Ladies are too sheltered. Experience is always valuable."

Lady Helena winced, both at this sentiment and its mocking reference.

Philippa quickly said: "It is certainly true that a lady's prime characteristic nowadays is her sensibility." She was rather proud of her calm reaction to Lord Charles's assault in the innyard.

"Most irritatingly,' said Lord Charles. "Women, begging your pardon, ladies, spend far too much of their time swooning and reading bad verse."

"Both endearing occupations," Lord Carlington said with a flash of humor.

"A woman can do great good in the world," Philippa said, "merely by remaining sensitive to the evils around her and by trying to correct them."

Lady Helena readily agreed and murmured: "She must be careful not to waste her time in frivolous activities."

"But Miss Winslow," Lord Carlington earnestly declared, "I would wish you and Lady Helena never to see the evils of the world."

"And, Miss Winslow, ladies often spend their time too prone to dispensing jellies and sage words to the deserving poor. Hardly very useful work. They seldom act and seldom truly mend any of the world's ills," Lord Charles said with some violence.

"You would wish women to extinguish fires, no doubt, Lord Charles? Society forbids them to take any such action! 'Action' is unladylike!" Philippa retorted.

Lord Charles was shaken, and Lady Helena put a restraining hand on her cousin's arm. Philippa hesitated, then gave a tinkly laugh.

"But I am placid and content as a lily of the field," she gushed.

Lord Charles, who had heard from his adoring brother how Philippa was bringing up her three younger sisters and brothers and had been managing a household since she was twelve, placed little credence in her statement, but the Earl found it most touching.

"That's precisely what you should be," he said warmly. "Few flowers could compete with you."

Philippa thanked the Earl nicely and wondered just what his brother was thinking. She did not deceive herself. Lord Charles's influence over his brother was great, and he could be a formidable enemy. He and Carlington, Philippa decided, were exact opposites. He had all the spirit and dash that Carlington lacked, but he had it in excess. While Carlington was unimaginative and unadventuresome, his brother was clearly a rackety sort of fellow, relying on a quick tongue and a handsome face to ease him out of scrapes. Philippa obscurely knew that she was being harsh, but that kiss in the innyard was, she assured herself, unforgivable.

The four conversed in monosyllables until they reached Philippa's home. She climbed down, assuring the Earl that now she had not forgotten she was bound to him for the first waltz at Lady Symington's ball, and ran to her room to ponder this new complication.

Lord Charles was thinking of it too, but, unlike Miss Winslow, he whistled gaily as he thought of the weeks in store. Whatever the outcome, watching the Earl of Carlington's courtship of Philippa Winslow, who was as lively as her admirer was dull, would certainly be amusing.

Chapter Six

Lord Carlington did not, after all, drive Lady Helena Prescott home. When she learned from him that his mother was at Blawith House, on one of her infrequent visits to the metropolis, she decided to ride on and call on the Marchioness. Honoria Moreland had been a great friend of Helena's mother and her mother's sister Adelaide, the cousin of Philippa who had married a German nobleman. Helena's mother had made an even better match, marrying the Duke of Hetford. She had died at Helena's birth, however, and Lady Helena had been raised abroad by her Aunt Adelaide. Lady Blawith had kindly offered to sponsor Helena at her coming-out, and it was from Blawith House on Grosvenor Street, rather than Hetford House in Cavendish Square, that Lady Helena, almost ten years before, had been presented to the world. It had not been a particularly successful presentation. Lady Helena, shy and tongue-tied, had not been popular even with so shy and tongue-tied a young gentleman as her patroness's eldest son. She had not married and, apparently content with her lot, lived alone with her aged father, engaging in good works. She remained on intimate terms with the Marchioness, but since Lady Blawith preferred, as she grew older, to spend most of the year on her country estate, they saw each other rarely.

Lady Blawith, indeed, had hoped to meet Lady Helena in London and greeted her with warmth.

"My dear Helena, I was just going to send a *billet* round to you! I am so glad Carlington brought you round. You may go, Carlington," she said peremptorily to her first-born. "Helena and I can have a comfortable cose much better with you out of the room."

Carlington had no choice but to obey his mother's imperiously pointing finger (in any lesser woman, lady Helena reflected, a pointed finger would have been a mark of ineradicable vulgarity) and meekly left his mother's boudoir.

The Marchioness then commanded Lady Helena to sit down and remove her bonnet. "And tell me all about your delightful cousin!"

Lady Helena boggled a little at this blunt request. Why was Lady Blawith interested in Philippa? she wondered. If Lord Charles had not discovered who the young lady he met in the innyard was until an hour ago, how could he have told his mother of his escapade? And he had certainly been unaware of Philippa's identity at the earlier *rencontre,* or, knowing she was a particular friend of his brother's, his behaviour, Lady Helena judged, would have been more circumspect.

Her unspoken query was soon answered.

"I've only met Philippa once," the Marchioness explained, "and I did like her, but now, you see, George has taken a fancy to her and I simply must see what it is all about! I can't remember him taking such a pronounced interest in a woman ever before. Quite unlike dear Charles!"

Lady Helena was shaken. This was the first she had heard of any attachment between Carlington—whom she had known since her *début*—and her cousin Philippa. She had seen them dance together a few times; that was all. It would be, of course, a brilliant match for Philippa, and, as she thought of it, Philippa would doubtless get along with the sometimes overpowering Marchioness. Yet, somehow, Lady Helena had never thought of stolid George Staunton marrying her lovely cousin, and the idea made her slightly uneasy. She was very fond of Philippa, but she was far from sure that Philippa appreciated Carlington's sterling qualities.

Lady Blawith interrupted Helena's reverie.

"What would you think of such a match, Helena? Would they suit? Carlington should marry someone soon—I'm sure he'll be happiest when surrounded by a wife and children who adore him, just like his father. Though James never had that, poor dear. At least he seems happy now, with adoring birds all around him. But Carlington needs a wife. Would Philippa Winslow do? Would she adore him? Carlington needs adoration, you know. Not love. Certainly not passion. Merely uncritical adoration."

"Philippa is not likely to be uncritical, I suppose," Lady Helena said cautiously. "She has a mind of her own. She respects Lord Carlington, of course . . ."

"Oh, dear! That doesn't sound promising. But perhaps you don't agree with me? About George's character, I mean."

Lady Helena had a sudden vision of a future spent arranging other people's marriages, advising mothers, and consoling lovelorn adolescents. That lay before her, she knew, as an elderly spinster—there was little else to look forward to. At least, she thought wryly, she had enough money to live on, and her birth, of course, gave her *entrée* everywhere. She could live quite happily and peacefully on into middle age, she supposed, but she did wish people would not ask her advice about marriage.

"How would I know?" she said in a spurt of anger. "I haven't the slightest idea whether they would be well-suited, and neither do you! They shall simply have to work it out for themselves!"

Her hot statement was not quite true, for Lady Helena was realizing that the more she thought about it, the less suitable the marriage seemed.

Lady Blawith, rather pleased than offended by Lady Helena's show of spirit, pointed out that the two young people did not want to be left alone to decide.

"Carlington will never do anything I advise against, Helena. He has the most endearingly malleable character! Like my husband. I write to James once a year telling him to stay in South America, and he does. Not at all like Charles! Why, George would never even go against Charles's advice! He holds us both in the greatest esteem!"

"All the more reason," Lady Helena angrily replied, "for you not to abuse that respect and filial obedience! You are far too fond of interfering!"

With that bit of plain speaking, Lady Helena picked up her bonnet and wished Lady Blawith a good day, leaving the Marchioness not a whit impressed by her last exhortation. Indeed, the Marchioness instantly turned her powerful mind to work out just why dear Helena was so upset and what could be done about it. The Marchioness was distracted from this agreeable task by the entrance of her younger son.

"Well, Mamma," Lord Charles said with a grin, "have you pumped Lady Helena dry of all her knowledge about the fascinating Miss Winslow?"

"Is she fascinating, Charles?"

"Very, *maman*." Lord Charles dropped a kiss on

his mother's brow and took his accustomed seat on her right.

"Carlington told us so last night," he continued.

"Not in so many words!" his mother expostulated.

"He said, I believe, that she was 'a most charming young lady,' adding that he was sure we would like her. I think that means he finds her fascinating—and he certainly seems enthralled when with her," Lord Charles chuckled.

"When with her? How do you know? You've never met the girl!"

"So I said last night, *chérie*, but this afternoon it has transpired that I was wrong."

"You've met her, you mean? What is she like?"

"I have met her, ma'am, on two separate occasions."

"Charles," his mother threatened, "I shall be seriously displeased if you do not at once tell me what you think of Miss Winslow! And when have you met her?"

"You mean Helena Prescott didn't tell you? How remiss of her, to be sure! But perhaps she was in a hurry."

"Yes, it was the most curious thing!" his mother said, momentarily diverted. "But what about Miss Winslow?"

"Well, Mother—" and Lord Charles told her the story of his *rencontre* at Watford. She was amused, as he had known she would be.

"You seem to like her," she commented pensively at the end of his recital. "But, liking aside, do you think she's good for George?"

"Yes, I do rather. She wakes him up a bit—makes him think of something other than politics. Any pretty woman could do that—"

"Not to Carlington!" his mother protested.

"No, I suppose not. But anyway, this Winslow girl's got something special. Charm, *esprit*. You will like her."

"I think so," she agreed. "I shall have to see more of this paragon. Carlington has objected so to all your *chères amies,* on principle, and he himself hasn't spoken to any women for years—I never thought to hear you two agree about any female!"

"If you attend Lady Symington's ball tonight you can see her and swell the chorus of praises, *maman.*"

"Not even your paragon could induce me ever to darken Aurelia Symington's doors again!" Lady Blawith roundly told him. "Her ballroom is perfumed like a palace in one of Byron's romances. Makes me sneeze!"

Lord Charles chuckled and took his leave.

Henry Francis Winslow did not disappoint his sister. He arrived in London with just enough time to wolf down a hasty meal and to don evening dress before escorting Philippa to Lady Symington's ball. She was not, however, properly grateful for his presence; she was preoccupied with other matters. The prospect of meeting Lord Charles again filled her with some trepidation, but also with a certain exhilaration. She put on a new gown for the ball, and she was delighted to find that the pearl and sapphire necklace that had been her mother's matched the deep blue of her satin gown perfectly. She was even more pleased when, as Petherton was hooking up the white lace overdress, a maid brought up flowers in a jeweled holder from Lord Carlington. Such attentiveness was a propitious sign, Philippa decided, and the snowdrops, as Henry Francis told her when they met downstairs, looked very elegant.

"I feel very elegant," Philippa rapturously sighed. "I feel elegant, and grown-up, and very charming. And proud to have such a handsome escort."

"Anyone would think, my dear, that you were a *débutante* awaiting her first ball."

"But that's how I do feel," Philippa exclaimed, her earlier *ennui* forgotten. "I'm just as excited as if this were my first ball, although I suppose I'm more confident now than I was then."

"You always were confident, Phil. An arrogant little girl!" her brother affectionately replied.

"Well, it isn't confidence in myself, Henry, it's confidence in the goodness of the world! Everything in it seems perfectly wonderful, including, of course, both you and me!"

"Quite," Henry Francis said crisply as he handed her into the carriage.

Lord and Lady Symington had spared no expense to make their ball a success. The champagne was of the finest quality, and the orchestra they had hired well above the average. The guests unusually brilliant and gay. Philippa Winslow was the gayest of all. She sparkled that evening. She was surrounded by admirers wherever she went. Philippa seemed the very embodiment of youth and joy as she laughed, danced, and bantered with the young men paying her court. She airily sent them off to procure lemonade for her or to ask one of the less successful ladies sitting dolefully among the chaperones for a dance, but did so with such charm that none of them minded. So austere a judge as the Princess Esterhazy commented to her friend Henry Luttrell that Miss Winslow was "positively scintillating," and Don Fernando de Santiago y Anandas watched Philippa all evening with doglike devotion.

Philippa was not gratified as she should have been by these marks of success. Lord Carlington did not seem to be present. As it grew late, and the orchestra, bidden by Lady Symington, struck up the first waltz, Philippa looked about her to see with whom she could dance. She had refused, of course, all other offers. If now Carlington were not to appear, she thought glumly, she would be well-served for her scheming and her vanity. She angrily scanned the vast room, jumping when she was suddenly addressed.

"My brother most sincerely begs your pardon, Miss Winslow. There is a debate of great importance in Parliament—he has been called to Westminster. He asked me take his place, which, I assure you, I am happy to do," Charles Staunton explained in a slightly mocking drawl.

Philippa heard all this with some horror. She was disappointed at losing Carlington's company, and she wasn't at all sure that a waltz with Lord Charles would prove a pleasant experience—the conversation might be embarrassing. On the other hand, it could not well be worse than hearing him make nasty references to their first meeting in front of other people, so Philippa smiled sweetly and took Lord Charles's proffered hand.

"I am so glad to see you, Lord Charles. One doesn't like to be left without a partner for the first waltz of the evening."

"No, I should imagine not. But surely, Miss Winslow, you could command any one of two dozen men here to dance with you. Don Fernando de Santiago, for example. He's watching you at this moment." Lord Charles deftly guided her to the center of the floor.

"Don Fernando did ask me," Philippa admitted, "but of course I was waiting for Lord Carlington. Do you know Don Fernando?"

"No, I have never met him, although my brother told me he had met him yesterday. George didn't think much of him, and I must say I agree. He looks the very picture of a Spanish *bourgeois*—a class we learned to distrust on the Peninsula."

They spoke for some moments about Lord Charles's war experiences. Philippa was acutely aware of his arm around her. It was a heady sensation and she decided she knew why the Patronesses of Almack's were so wary about this new dance.

"Have you exhausted your store of novels yet, Miss Winslow?" Lord Charles abruptly asked. "Or have you had only time for the merest trifling—say, two or three books—in the time since my brother and I left you?"

Philippa, fortunately, recognized this as a joke. "Hardly, sir. I had only reached the first swoon in *The Enigmatic Marquis* when I was forced to stop to dress for the evening!"

"What a pity, Miss Winslow," Lord Charles replied in the same serious tone. "Surely you could have given up the ball—enjoyable as it is—to learn the outcome of the blushing Constanza's adventure."

"Not Constanza! Zenobia!"

"And had she swooned when confronted with an apparition?"

"Truly, Lord Charles, you should write one of these yourself. Your insight into the subtleties of the novel is remarkable!"

"A dubious compliment, Miss Winslow. And I fear it would be ignoble for a former servant of the King to turn his hand to such a task."

"A great talent is being lost to the world in your refusal, Lord Charles! A very great talent, I am certain."

"You almost persuade me. Perhaps I shall write a story of the people here tonight."

"Yes, that would be admirable. One could, in exposing all society's faults and foibles, have a *succès de scandale*."

"A delightful idea. I would enjoy so much telling the truth about this frivolous crowd."

"The truth, Lord Charles? Surely that's dangerous. And would doubtless prove unpopular!"

"Ah, but how invigorating! I would take great pleasure in informing the world just who is quarrelling with whom and who is whose light-of-love and—"

"Lord Charles!" Philippa severely exclaimed.

"I am sorry, Miss Winslow," Lord Charles said contritely. "I've been out of proper society for so long that I've forgotten how to speak to a lady."

He looked genuinely embarrassed. Philippa suddenly felt sorry she had put him in this position—it somehow seemed to be important he didn't think her a fool.

"You certainly can't be very good at society *on-dits,* then," she smoothly said. "Perhaps you should stay with a simple tale of horror and adventure."

"No, I could commission someone else to write a society novel for me. Even if it didn't include the latest rumours, it would be so amusing to see, for example, the Princess Esterhazy as a frightened and *naïve* heroine."

"Or Don Fernando as a dashing hero," Philippa contributed.

"Or even Prinny himself!"

"As a sinister villain!"

The thought of the Prince Regent in the guise of the pupil of the Borgias or, at least, the Jesuits who thwarted the heroine's hopes for happiness in all the novels of the day proved irresistibly funny to them both, and, laughing, they parted as the waltz ended. Philippa agreed to meet Lord Charles for dinner. She found herself, as she waltzed with some intolerably callow young man, looking forward to midnight, when the food would be served.

After the callow youth, she danced, in rapid succession, with a noted dandy, who asked her where she had procured her snowdrops, her kindly, if inarticulate, host, and several admirers whom she did not even notice. It was not, she assured herself, that she only attracted dull men, but that the majority of men in London were dull. It was with a sense of relief that she greeted even the prosy Don Fernando when he returned to her side.

"May I have this dance, Miss Winslow? Having spent an hour in bitterest exile from your so-warming

Philippa

presence, surely I may be granted that slight indulgence."

"Of course you may have this dance," Philippa said graciously, ignoring the glares of the gentleman (who was, she feared, in his cups) to whom she was promised.

Don Fernando did not miss the other gentleman's angry looks and drew from them a misleading conclusion. If Miss Winslow were willing to break her word in order to dance with him, she must indeed be fond of him. Don Fernando, unknown to Philippa, had also been imbibing heavily of the excellent champagne, and he was enflamed by Philippa's unexpected cordiality. Before they had gone ten yards across the floor, Philippa found herself swept onto Lady Symington's elegant terrace and there, pressed against the ivy that entwined the marble balustrade, being ardently asked to marry the man kneeling at her feet.

"You are to me, Miss Winslow, the ideal of womanly goodness and perfection. Will you become my bride? I beg of you, I implore you, to say yes!"

The scene was a romantic one, as Philippa observed in one part of her mind. The moonlight streamed down on the marble, making the white lace of her dress shine as if it were jeweled, and Don Fernando, his arms outstretched in entreaty, clearly believed, at the moment, in what he said. She was, nevertheless, horridly embarrassed. She had miscalculated, not thinking he was ready yet to propose to her. She did not want to marry Don Fernando if she could marry Lord Carlington, and she tried, as gently as possible, to turn down the Spaniard's obliging offer. "I am sorry, Don Fernando, but—"

"But why?" Don Fernando asked in outrage. "I will give you everything, everything I have."

"I don't think, Don Fernando, that I can love you or that I can marry you. I am deeply sensible of the honour you do me, and, while my mind is irrevocably made up, I do hope that we can remain friends," Philippa said, in just the words a young lady should use

63

on such an occasion. Don Fernando, while disappointed, was not surprised. Englishwomen were notoriously cold, and he knew that such a beauty as Philippa Winslow might well require some reflection before giving up her untrammeled life.

"I must implore you, ma'am, to think on my proposal for a longer time. Perhaps—"

"No, I assure, Don Fernando," Philippa interpolated, "I'm quite sure of my decision."

Don Fernando was still not too cast down. "Very well, Miss Winslow. I need not even tell you that a word at any time will bring me to your side."

"Thank you, Don Fernando. I am greatly flattered."

Don Fernando bowed and left her. Philippa stood on the terrace, pressing her hands to her burning cheeks. She was considerably shaken, although she didn't know why. Why should she be? she asked herself. She now had precisely what she wanted. Don Fernando could wait in reserve, and, if she failed with Lord Carlington, she could summon him back. Then she chided herself for being so odiously practical. She did not think Don Fernando was seriously in love with her; but it still seemed cruel to scheme so coldly about someone's kind offer. She came to herself with a start, realizing that it was time to go down for dinner. She re-entered the ballroom, hoping no one would notice her flushed cheeks. She was soon found by Lord Charles, who, if he did notice her agitation, was too well-bred to comment on it.

Chapter Seven

Lord Charles steered Philippa down the broad staircase that led to the dining-room, where a cold collation had been set up. Philippa was still distraught, but she idly wondered why Lord Charles was parrying all their friends' requests to join them. He apparently wanted to be alone with her, although she did not dare try to fathom why. She mutely let herself be led, after Lord Charles had given her a plate of cold meats and a glass of champagne, to a secluded alcove just outside the main room.

"I must apologize to you, Miss Winslow, for my appalling behaviour a few days ago," he began.

Philippa coughed deprecatingly.

"There is no need, Lord Charles," she said with dignity. "Perhaps it would be easiest if we forgot the incident altogether."

"That's an admirable solution. I'm glad to hear your memory is so accommodating."

He lifted his champagne glass.

"To our first meeting, which never occurred."

Philippa toasted with him, giggling.

"I believe I've met your father," Lord Charles said, frowning.

"Yes, he mentioned it."

"Your father is then Rupert Winslow?"

"Indubitably."

"You're not much like him. Or perhaps you are."

"I beg your pardon?"

"You, er, have his charm of manner," Lord Charles explained in some embarrassment.

Philippa took pity on him. "But I don't have my father's devil-may-care attitude. Is that what you mean?"

"Precisely. Although it would be hard to be as insouciant as your endearing father. My father is excruciatingly dull."

"Father *is* endearing. But he's far too reckless to run a household. Henry Francis—that's my brother—and I are forced to be upright and responsible. Someone has to think ahead."

"Quite," Lord Charles agreed.

He put down his glass and looked at her measuringly. There was a moment of silence.

"Are you going to marry my brother?" he abruptly fired at her.

"I beg your pardon!" Philippa stammered.

"Oh, I know, he hasn't asked you, but I want to know if you'd accept him," Lord Charles said impatiently.

Champagne gave Philippa courage.

"Yes. Yes, I would. I have a very high regard for your brother—I find him quite delightful."

"You find Carlington delightful?" Lord Charles drawled. "You interest me."

Philippa chuckled in spite of herself. "Delightful" had been the wrong word. Then she stiffened. "Why, sir, are you so impertinent as to ask me this? What do you mean by it?"

"No, don't get on a high horse. I like you, and I'd like you to marry George. Don't look so astounded—I was merely curious about your feelings. It's a good match for you, I suppose. And you deserve it—with that father of yours. I think George will ask you, you know; he admires you very much."

Philippa, who was indeed totally astounded by this conversation, said, "I am of course flattered to hear that. But what concern is it of yours?"

"Oh, not the least in the world," Lord Charles admitted. "I merely think that it would be a good marriage. It would help you considerably and you'd like being the Marchioness of Blawith, I daresay. And it would wake George up a bit to be married to you."

Philippa laughed. She couldn't believe this absurd conversation was taking place, but she was enjoying it nonetheless. And she was elated by Lord Charles' prediction.

"You make me feel like some peculiar electrical shock!"

"Not at all a bad thing to be where Carlington is concerned. But I just wanted you to know I'm your friend. And that may make a difference. George has always been scrupulously aware of his importance as the head of the family. His marriage, he feels, is a dynastic alliance, and he'll never take so significant a step without consulting Mother and me. Father doesn't matter of course; he's too far away. He'll never bother to venture an opinion. Don't worry, Mother'll like you—you're very much alike."

Philippa accept this with a startling rush of gratitude and joy.

"Very well, sir. I'm very glad. I do hope," she shamelessly said, "I do hope I marry your brother."

"So you will, Miss Winslow. I feel confident. Ah,

they're striking up another waltz. Will you dance with me?"

Philippa curtseyed. "With pleasure, my noble ally!"

The papers announced the next morning that Lady Symington's ball had been a great success. Lord Charles, striding home that evening, whistling through the darkened streets, would have agreed wholeheartedly. Philippa, with a drowsy smile on her face, thought so too and told Henry Francis as much during their ride home.

"Did you enjoy yourself?" she inquired.

"Tolerably. I danced with Cousin Helena. Did you see her? She looked somewhat *distraite*."

"Helena? She seemed quite as usual this afternoon," Philippa abstractedly replied.

"What did you think of the ball? You look aglow."

"Oh, I am, Henry. It was a lovely evening."

"Any particular cause?"

Philippa shrugged. "Not really," she lied.

Henry Francis regarded her with suspicion, but did not question further.

Philippa's glow was noticed by all of London soon enough. She was radiantly happy that spring and everyone knew it. It was not difficult to guess that the cause of her mood was Lord Carlington's marked attentions. He was clearly much taken with her, but, even so, her joy seemed excessive. She dashed about the city, never stopping. Venetian breakfasts, drives to Richmond, the wild-beast show at Exeter Exchange, *Macbeth* at the Orpheum, fireworks and masquerades at Vauxhall, expeditions to Greenwich and Windsor, even dinners with the Prince Regent at Carlton House; Philippa was everywhere that spring. Lord Carlington spent most of his time, however, battling in Parliament. True, he spent more time with Miss Winslow than with anyone else, but that hardly seemed enough to cause her jubilation. Carlington sent his brother to escort Philippa as his delegate quite often, but that, while an encouraging sign, also did not seem to justify Philippa's radiance. Helena Prescott got very tired of continually explaining to acquaintances that even she could not fathom her cousin's mood. Philippa herself, indeed, didn't know the reason for her happiness. All she knew was that every day seemed like a jewel, and each was more precious and sparkling than the one before. Clarissa had recovered, and Sir Rupert was behaving with more than usual circumspection, anxious not to injure his daughter's chances for a noble alliance, but Philippa hardly noticed that. For the first time in her life, her first thoughts were not of her family and household affairs. She mentioned as much to Lord Charles one morning when he came to pick her up for their customary morning ride in Hyde Park.

"That shows you're ready to set up a household of your own! Isabella, if I'm thinking of the right one, is surely old enough to take over the responsibility of this one, and there's nothing wrong in your thinking of yourself for once."

"But I think of myself all the time! How else could I be planning to marry?"

"True enough. George asked me to tell you he'd call at noon or so."

"Ah, how kind of him. I shall have to change clothes."

Lord Charles ignored the suggestion that a dress good enough to wear for a ride with *him* was not good enough for a meeting with his brother.

"But your frock is charming, Miss Winslow!"

"It's two years old!"

"It's still charming. A two-year-old child is much more charming than a newborn infant."

"Yes," Philippa agreed. "How do you know?"

"Intuition." Lord Charles smiled. "I don't think I've ever seen a two-year-old."

"You're fortunate. They *look* charming!" she darkly said.

"Robin's nine, isn't he?"

"Yes. But his manners have only slightly improved in the last seven years. He was atrociously rude to your brother yesterday."

"But why?"

"Carlington had asked Robin last week if he knew any speech of Fox's by heart. Poor Robin didn't, of course, although he did offer Cicero."

"*Quo usque tandem abutere Catalina,*" Lord Charles solemnly intoned.

"Precisely. That wasn't good enough for your brother, so he promised Robin a gift if he'd learn one of Fox's. Robin was easily bribed by the offer and has been studiously conning the shortest one he could find. He's addressed us all in orotund periods for days. He talks like the great man himself."

"Better Fox than Burke," Lord Charles interjected.

"I suppose so, but either sounds most inappropriate when he's speaking through a nine-year-old boy. Anyway, Carlington came to call Saturday and heard the whole thing through. He patted Robin on the head and swore to bring his gift in a few days."

"Yes, he told me about this. He went to great trouble to select a proper present."

"That's just the problem. Can you imagine giving a child Locke's *Treatises?* Edifying and all that—I have no doubt Mr. Fox himself would approve. But Robin was sorely disappointed. He was barely civil."

"George obviously thought the lad was truly inspired by our grand political tradition. I'm surprised it wasn't Coke on the common law!"

Philippa laughed. "Robin expected tin soldiers, I believe. I told him it was a compliment to be given an adult gift, but I'm afraid he didn't see it that way."

"Good God, no. I'm not sure I should welcome the book myself—even at my age."

"Well, it is a lovely book, but I admit I can think of many things I would rather have. It all worked out well, though. Henry Francis clearly coveted the volume, so Robin offered him it in exchange for tin soldiers."

"Clever lad! I hope Henry Francis took him up on it."

"Gladly, and we all sighed in relief. But don't tell your brother!"

"I give you my word of honour, Miss Winslow."

"I can always rely on you." Philippa smiled.

Chapter Eight

Visitors to Hetford House were rare. Not, of course, that they were discouraged. On the contrary, Helena Prescott always received callers with the utmost courtesy. The Duke of Hetford seldom descended from the fastness of his library, but his daughter would stop whatever she was doing—answering letters from charitable organizations, going over menus with the housekeeper, playing cribbage with her father—to entertain her guests. If they were fortunate, they were in time to stay for tea. Tea at Hetford House was a grand affair. (*"Three* different cakes, and crumpets, and muffins, and bread-and-butter! And cucumber sandwiches! And watercress!" Isabella Winslow had reported to her younger sister and brother after the first time Philippa had taken her to call on their cousin Helena.) It was seldom, though, that Lady Helena had even a young cousin to entertain. She was, after all, a spinster, almost an ape-leader. Her second, third, and even fourth seasons were long behind

her, and old maids did not participate in the delights of
the London season. She was invited to the larger balls
each year. She attended an occasional concert or *musi-
cale*. In the autumn and winter there were house-parties
at the homes of relatives. She contrived to rub along
very well, she told herself, even if she did not have the
dozens of gentlemen callers her cousin Philippa took
for granted. In her youth Lady Helena had been thrown
into a panic by the sound of the doorknocker. She had
been awkward and silent, too tall, and badly dressed.
There *had* been gentlemen callers back then, but they
had seldom enjoyed themselves, and Lady Helena had
hated the whole business. She had learned to dress better, and she had mastered the polite formulas that
dealt with visitors. She actually liked having visitors
now. Only her friends called on her now, and she
greeted them with quiet composure. She moved grace-
fully, pouring the tea and ringing the bell for more
sandwiches. Philippa, watching her one afternoon in early
April, would not have credited for a moment the sorry
stories Lady Blawith, had she been so cruel as to do
so, could have told about Lady Helena's unhappy
début.

"I like that frock, Helena," she said unexpectedly.
"Austrian blue becomes you."

"Thank you—I'm very fond of the colour. And
it's a change from Saxe-Coburg crimson!"

"I like crimson, but it is getting tedious! Do you
know, I saw Saxe-Coburg crimson *slippers* for sale in the
Pantheon bazaar last week!"

"How extraordinary!"

"My loyalty to the House of Hanover," Philippa
said seriously, "is as profound as anyone else's, and I
wish Princess Charlotte very well with her German
bridegroom, but we have been wearing crimson for three
months now and I cannot but hope that someone else

in the Royal Family is betrothed, very soon, to, say, a prince of Norway whose colour is cerulean blue!"

"Philippa, my dear, I don't think the colour of the Kings of Norway is blue, and in any case that would be a most unstrategic alliance!"

"I was quizzing you, coz! I don't think there *are* any Norwegian princes!"

"It is not really a subject for levity, dearest. Now that the Corsican has been dealt with and the governments of Europe must be reconstituted on legitimate lines, the arranging of England's alliances is a grave responsibility. Such marriages as the Princess's can change the map of Europe."

"Hardly, Helena! Saxe-Coburg was not, after all, a particularly adventuresome choice. I have nothing against Prince Leopold, but one must admit that the success of his wooing was not surprising! He was the obvious, safest bridegroom for the Princess. If she were to marry an Austrian, now, then I might see some sense in altering the map of Europe!"

Helena stared at her cousin. "Philippa Winslow! You are not suggesting a *Catholic* alliance! My dear!"

"Merely a supposition, coz!"

"I should hope so! And I pray you don't repeat it to anyone who does not know your, er, volatile temperament."

Philippa giggled. "I thought everyone knew about my volatile temperament. But do you know, I told Lord Carlington last night that it was a pity the erstwhile King of Rome is still an infant—it would have been so nice to have ended the war with a general alliance and a grand marriage!"

"Buonaparte's son!" Lady Helena gasped. "Philippa, you are quizzing me again!"

"No, I'm not, honestly! Lord Carlington stared at me and didn't say anything at all, but Lord Charles pointed out that we could have had a grand *betrothal*— that is, if we had a baby princess. Maybe Charlotte will have one quickly. A betrothal in their cradles would be a lovely gesture. So Gothic!"

"I cannot think," Lady Helena replied stiffly, "that so high-minded a statesman as the Earl appreciated your frivolous suggestion!"

"Well, Lord Charles did, and Henry Francis chuckled! Then Carlington realized it was a pleasantry and complimented me on it," Philippa said with a mocking tone in her voice.

Lady Helena took exception to this. "Really, Philippa! I begin to think you quite rag-mannered. You were being much too forward when all the gentlemen there knew much more about the subject than you did. Ladies should never discuss politics."

"Cousin Helena, you can't call that a political discussion! And I'm not at all sure they knew more about the subject than I do! Henry Francis, at least, only reads the *Gentleman's Magazine* and the *Edinburgh Review,* and I read those just as carefully as he does!"

"You should not," Lady Helena interjected.

"And I'm sure I know more about Gothic betrothals than any of them did! I've read Froissart and, for that matter, Malory. And I'm sure none of them have."

"Oh, Philippa," Lady Helena sighed. "Your father should never have let you run loose in his library. I don't know whether it's worse to read mediaeval chronicles or marble-covered novels, but both are improper reading for a young girl!"

"You're forgetting the *Edinburgh Review!*" Philippa put in quite imperturbably.

"That is the most improper. I wonder your brother permits you!"

"He doesn't know." Philippa grinned. "And don't worry, nobody else does either! I hardly go around town quoting King Arthur and Sir Lancelot!"

"Gracious, the peculiar books in the library at Wimcombe!" Lady Helena said with a shudder.

"It's the fault of my antiquarian great-grandfather. He collected them all."

"I am glad the library at Durwick, while extensive enough, contains few volumes unsuitable for a lady's perusal!"

"Helena, how can you possibly know?" Philippa inquired. "I refuse to believe you've read them all! I've seen the library at Durwick! Even I, in my misspent youth, never read that many books!"

"Oh, Phil!" Lady Helena laughed and changed the subject. "Where were you last night, anyway? It sounds like an agreeable party."

"Oh, it was! Lord Carlington took his mother and me to the theatre. I like Lady Blawith so much! She's quite unlike the Earl!"

"No, it's Charles who takes after his mother," Lady Helena agreed. "He attended too?"

"Yes, he decided to at the last minute. And Henry Francis escorted me, so it was quite a cosy family party."

"What did you see?"

"*Measure for Measure* at Covent Garden. Carlington's choice, of course. Lord Charles promised to take me to *School for Scandal* next week."

"What a gratifying rush of activity!"

"To be sure!"

"Did you enjoy the play? It's my favourite of Shakespeare's works."

"Not mine. I don't think the language is as beautiful or as touching as in his earlier plays. And I can't say I'm much drawn to the heroine."

"Truly? I think she's most admirable."

"Oh, admirable, of course, but compared to Rosalind, or Viola, or Beatrice!"

"My dear, you cannot expect wit from the heroine of so serious a play as *Measure for Measure!*"

"No, but one can miss it! And I didn't like Miss O'Neill at all in the part."

"I've never seen her, but she's quite highly spoken of, isn't she?"

"Oh, yes," said Philippa, momentarily impatient with her cousin's ignorance of the contemporary theatre. "But she's much better in comedy. I look forward to seeing her as Lady Teazle next week!"

"Yes, that sounds lovely," Lady Helena coolly replied. She shocked herself with her sudden resentment of Philippa, who calmly accepted all these gay activities as her due. Philippa had never known the humiliation of sitting, unwanted, at the side of a ballroom; Philippa's doorknocker was never silent; Philippa was never lonely.

"What's wrong?" Philippa asked, sensing her cousin's change of mood. "Am I boring you, gabbling on like this? Nothing more tedious, I know, dear, than conversations one wasn't part of! I'll take my leave."

"No, Philippa, it wasn't that. You are always amusing. I enjoy hearing your tales of fine London doings."

Philippa did not miss the bitterness in Lady Helena's voice.

"When were you last at the theatre, coz?" she abruptly asked.

Lady Helena smiled. "It's been four years, I think. An unmarried woman can't go alone even to the opera."

"Then you will of course accompany us next week." Philippa ignored her cousin's objections. "Although I don't know how fond you are of *School for Scandal*. You don't usually read comedies, but that's all the better! Make a change for you. And Mr. Sheridan is simply inimitable. D'you know, he's supposed to be dreadfully ill now? He must be quite old. I remember being told in my cradle about his elopement with the beautiful Miss Linley! Father knew Mrs. Sheridan, I believe. Father would."

Philippa paused for breath, contemplating her father's general range of acquaintances, and Lady Helena was able to speak.

"Phil, you can't simply go around inviting other people to be a member of your party with Lord Charles. What will he think?"

Philippa laughed. "He'll think it's a splendid idea! He's known you ever since you came back from Bonn, after all."

"That doesn't mean he wants to take me to the theatre."

"He is my friend. And so are you. That means we shall have a delightful evening. Perhaps Carlington will come too, if he's not too busy at the House."

"My dear, when Lord Carlington has already given up one evening this week to escort you to the theatre, you can hardly expect him to do so again. In the interests of the nation! He is an extremely busy man."

"It would be in the interests of the nation if all the members of Parliament and the Cabinet would relax now and then."

"Like the Regent?" Lady Helena acidly inquired.

"Relaxing doesn't *necessarily* mean losing all sense of propriety, Helena!"

Both ladies laughed, as the ormolu clock on the mantlepiece chimed. Philippa hastily finished her cucumber sandwich and put down her cup of tea.

"Oh, dear, I'm supposed to be home at this moment. I have to help Jarvis interview a girl who wants to be a housemaid. He should be able to do it, of course, but he's getting so old! Says he doesn't understand this younger generation, and especially not London girls! So I promised I would help—rather than rely on his failing powers of discrimination!"

"But Philippa, you need a housekeeper to do that sort of work!"

"You don't know, coz, how great an extravagance

79

this new housemaid is!" Philippa stood up and smiled at Lady Helena. "It's rather nasty being poor."

Lady Helena swiftly crossed the room and kissed her cousin.

"I don't doubt it. I'm sorry, Philippa. And I'm glad you can enjoy yourself most of the time."

Lady Helena rang for the tea-things to be cleared after Philippa had left. Lady Helena sat down to think. Philippa was right, of course. Philippa had said that in self-pity—she was further removed from self-pity than anyone Helena knew—but to make her cousin think for a moment. Helena had been indulging in self-pity. And unjustifiably. Philippa might be a gazetted beauty, but she was in a desperate and uncomfortable situation, with little money and a thoroughly unreliable father. Philippa's life was scarcely devoted to frivolities: She was endlessly worried about her younger brother and sisters and took very good care of them. If Philippa married the Earl of Carlington, as, Lady Helena had to admit, was looking more and more likely, it would be for the sake of his money, but how could anyone condemn her for that? She needed the money and deserved it. It was silly to envy Philippa. Lady Helena couldn't imagine paying calls, as Philippa had done today, in last year's frock. No, the only thing she could fairly envy Philippa was her freedom from self-pity, her gaiety, her energy, her youth. Philippa had grave troubles, but she had the courage to face them. Lady Helena uneasily reflected that she would never have Philippa's resilience, Philippa's courage. For some reason Lady Helena's mind turned to the Earl of Carlington. She wondered if he had ever felt this way, if he had ever envied his younger brother's gaiety, zest, and reckless courage.

Hard upon her thoughts, the butler entered. "The Earl of Carlington," he announced.

Lady Helena was surprised, but rose placidly to

greet her visitor, and asked him if he would like some tea. "I can easily have a new tray brought in."

"No, no. Thank you. How are you, Helena? My mother has been asking after you."

"She is still in town, then? I haven't spoken to her for several weeks."

"You must dine with us some evening, then."

"I should be delighted, George. How is Charles? I have not seem him either for some time."

"Ah, Charles is enjoying himself extremely. Glad to be home, I expect. Mother and I were a little worried, you know, that he wouldn't quite hit it off with society."

"Oh, but he seems to! Philippa tells me she sees him everywhere."

"Yes, he's a great friend of Miss Winslow. They chatter away like brother and sister."

"How nice."

"Yes. I am pleased. Indeed . . . Helena, may I speak to you frankly?"

"Of course, George. We have known each other so long."

"And I must tell you, Helena, that I have always had the deepest respect for your character and judgement. It is for that reason that I wish your opinion on a delicate matter."

"Yes, George?"

Lord Carlington cleared his throat several times, stood up, and crossed the room. He stood at the window, fingering the thick damask curtains. He turned abruptly.

"What can you tell me about your cousin Rupert Winslow?"

"He's my mother's cousin, actually," Lady Helena explained. She was startled by this inquiry and could only surmise that Lord Carlington had heard some unsavoury gossip. She smiled. It was characteristic of the Earl to ask her. He would have been much better off consulting some gentleman of Sir Rupert's generation. *She* could tell the Earl little. First she ventured a question of her own.

"Why do you want to know, George?"

Lord Carlington cleared his throat again. "Er, Helena, I am sure you will felicitate me when I tell you I have the hope of asking your young cousin to become my wife."

Lady Helena had foreseen this, of course, although she hadn't expected Lord Carlington to confide in her. She didn't like the idea, she admitted to herself. Philippa was incurably frivolous. She would never properly appreciate the significance of Lord Carlington's political activities. Philippa didn't love Lord Carlington, Helena was very sure of that. That was understandable, and didn't matter too much in a society marriage, but Philippa didn't respect the Earl either. He was infatuated with her, but Lady Helena could only think that Philippa was not really the sort of woman to make him happy. But Lady Helena shook herself. Philippa deserved this marriage. And, in any case, Lady Helena had very little to do with it.

"I am delighted to hear this, George," she said steadily. "Philippa is one of my dearest friends and I count you one as well. Nothing could please me more than to see the two of you truly happy."

Lord Carlington smiled. "And you must see, Helena, why I am asking about her father. Charles and I just met Sir Rupert. He was leaving *Watier's!* Charles is, I realize, a member of the club, although I do not believe he goes there often, but for a gentleman of Sir Rupert's age to belong to such a notorious gambling club is most improper! Why, I believe the stakes there are often as high as five hundred guineas! And what I find more disturbing than that, we met Sir Rupert in the company of the Earl of Barrymore!"

"Goodness!" Lady Helena politely murmured.

"I was shocked, I may say *appalled,* by this *ren-*

contre. And to make it worse, Winslow insisted on speaking to us. I would simply have raised my hat and walked on. It does not do for a man in my position to consort with such as the Earl of Barrymore."

"No, indeed."

"Charles, of course, thought it very humourous. He actually accepted, in my name, Sir Rupert's invitation to a card-party Thursday night! Thank God—oh, I beg your pardon, my dear—it shall be a family evening. Just young Winslow, his father, Charles, and I. Charles seemed to think it might be amusing. And it's not as if I have the time to spare!"

"You could always cry off, because of your press of business," Lady Helena timidly suggested.

Lord Carlington smiled at her gratefully. "No, Helena, I can't do that. I accepted the invitation, or rather Charles did. It will be a most unpleasant evening, but I can't renege on it now. Not when I'm planning to ask the man for his daughter's hand in marriage. Wouldn't be courteous. But I must say, Helena, I'm worried about this whole set-up. There's something havey-cavey about Rupert Winslow, and I don't mind saying it bothers me. I can't afford, in my position, to have a notorious father-in-law. If he were involved in a scandal—well, it would ruin my chances of the Cabinet when we return to power. Look how William Lamb's hurt by his wife! He'll never return to politics!"

"Caro Lamb is really the most shameless woman! And I cannot condone Lord Byron's conduct either! Poetic genius does not excuse public immorality, and only a fool like Sally Jersey would think it did. My heart quite bleeds for Lady Byron. Such an estimable woman!"

Lord Carlington had precisely the same sentiments on this subject and permitted himself to be distracted.

"Yes, one can only be glad that Lady Jersey's ill-considered attempt to restore him to public favour last week did not succeed!"

"I quite agree. The audacity of inviting him to Al-

mack's! Philippa admires Lord Byron's poetry greatly, but
—thank heaven—she behaved properly and left as soon
as he entered!"

"How that man dared enter Almack's! As if any
honest woman would speak to him! Ponsonby tells me he
is rumoured to be leaving the country, and one must,
my dear Helena, be profoundly grateful for that!"

"Yes, indeed."

Despite Lady Helena's attempt to distract him, Lord
Carlington returned inexorably to his original subject.
"But you see, don't you, why I am worried about Sir
Rupert? It wouldn't matter if he went bankrupt, say—that
could be hushed up—but to be seen with Barrymore!
And to play at Watier's! Even that could hurt me."

Lady Helena reflected that the Earl was quite right.
Sir Rupert Winslow might declare politicians to be a dull
lot, but they were eminently well-behaved. Twenty-five
years ago, Fox could live openly with his mistress, but
now the utmost probity was demanded of the representa-
tives of the nation. The Whigs were in enough trouble,
tainted by their association with the disgraced wife of the
Prince Regent, as even so uninformed an observer as Lady
Helena knew, so that they would never trust a man involved in open scandal. And, as Lady Helena knew from
her Aunt Adelaide's stories, Rupert Winslow was all too
likely, if he were in trouble, to involve every member of
his family in open scandal. Yet, for Philippa's sake, she
tried to reassure the Earl.

"I wouldn't worry about it, George. *Your* reputation
is unblemished, as is Philippa's. Surely that would outweigh any other consideration."

"I hope so."

"And," Lady Helena went on consolingly, "any misdeeds on Sir Rupert's part are wholly conjectural. He's
not the most sober of men, perhaps, George, but he hasn't
done anything *scandalous*."

"So Charles reminds me. He says Sir Rupert will behave with the utmost circumspection once he realizes how important it is to my future, and his daughter's and the nation's, that there be no scandal."

Lady Helena privately thought that Lord Carlington was overstating his case a bit, but only said: "Well, then. You value your brother's opinion. And I'm sure he knows more about such things than I do."

"My brother has only been in England for a few weeks, after all, Helena. But you're right. I can always trust Charles. And I must admit I am singularly reluctant to press any acquaintance as to Sir Rupert's reputation. It savours of distrust."

"You could try, if you are so worried, George."

"It's not necessary. Charles, of course, will tell me if there is any real gossip. He always knows all the stories. I have faith in Charles."

"And I am sure he merits it, George."

Lord Carlington, comforted, took his leave. Lady Helena went upstairs for her daily card game with her father. She wanted Philippa to make a good match, she assured herself. This was a splendid match, and she must be happy for her young cousin. Sir Rupert was a sad rake, no doubt, but she could not believe his behaviour would be such as to seriously jeopardize Lord Carlington's political future. Lady Helena was always ready to think the best of people, and she was sure that Sir Rupert's faults had been grossly exaggerated. As she knocked on the door of her father's library, it occurred to her how nice it was that Philippa had found a friend in Lord Charles Staunton. Not surprising—the two of them were very much alike—but certainly pleasant for Philippa. And very useful.

Chapter Nine

Charles Staunton, indeed, was surprised at how nice he was being. He smiled ruefully as he looked at the two children squashed beside him in his curricle.

"If you kick your brother, Clarissa, you will be set down in the middle of the Park with no means of transportation home," he warned severely.

Clarissa giggled. "Philippa would be sure to ride by in a few days and she would save me," she pointed out.

"By then the birds would have covered you with leaves, like the Babes in the Wood," Robin contributed.

"You *need* to be kicked!"

Lord Charles interrupted the squabble. "There is not, properly speaking, room in this carriage for more than two people, and I foresee that I will soon regret succumbing to your blandishments! But I'm sure you don't just want to drive around."

"Behind such a smashing pair! I could do it all day!"

"Well, I couldn't," Clarissa informed her brother.

She flashed her most winning smile at Lord Charles. "I think we should go somewhere."

"Would ices at Gunther's suit you?" Lord Charles asked.

"Rather!" exclaimed Robin.

"Oh, yes," Clarissa sighed. "It is fortunate we saw you drive up. And that Philippa wasn't able to accompany you."

"From your point of view, my girl! I don't even remember asking you two in her stead."

"You didn't," Robin graciously told him. "But I'm sure you're enjoying yourself now that we suggested it. *Everybody* likes ices at Gunther's!"

"What is your sister doing? Jarvis told me she was busy with household matters, and I was so overawed I didn't dare press further."

"She's interviewing a new housemaid," Robin explained. "I heard Petherton talking about it this morning."

Lord Charles whistled softly between his teeth. He hadn't realized the Winslow finances did not run to a housekeeper. That was interesting—and he felt sorry for Philippa.

"Look, children!" he exclaimed. "There's Prinny's carriage. The dark-red one coming toward us."

The children craned their heads to catch a glimpse of the Prince Regent. The heavy, low-slung coach passed by them. The portly gentleman inside, glancing out the window at that moment, politely lifted his hat. Clarissa and Robin were overwhelmed.

"That was gracious, I must say," said Lord Charles. "I wouldn't have thought he'd remember me."

"You've met him?" Robin gasped.

"I was in his old regiment, you see. Donkey's years after he'd left, of course, but he reviews the troops now and then. Pays attention to the officers."

"That was Beau Brummell's regiment, too," Clarissa said. "Do you know him?"

"Ten years my senior, I'm afraid. But like your sister, I've met the Beau at parties. Your sister's danced with him twice, I believe."

"Goodness! Philippa never told us that!"

"She doesn't like to boast, I expect."

"Like you," Robin said. "That's why you never told us you were in the Hussars."

"Not just the Hussars, cawker! I was in the 10th!"

"Is that the best?"

"Best regiment in the Army, of course!"

"Oh." Robin digested this. "Did you see any grand battles?"

Lord Charles laughed. "There was a little skirmish in Belgium last year."

Clarissa was embarrassed for her brother. "He was at Waterloo, stoopid. Philippa told me."

Robin's eyes grew very wide. He did not permit Lord Charles to talk of anything else for the rest of the afternoon. Usually Lord Charles disliked talking about his Army experiences, but Robin and Clarissa were so impressed, and so ingenous, that he quite enjoyed himself, and even, after Gunther's, took them for a long ride through the Park. It was the fashionable hour; the children preened themselves to be seen by all the world riding with such a noted military hero.

Philippa was looking out the window of the drawing-room for them as they drove up. She ran to meet them, in time to hear Lord Charles finish a story.

"And the next day Arthur Hill announced that Lord Wellesley—as he was then—did not approve of the use of umbrellas during enemy action. They looked too silly. Tony complained, though. Said that old one of his had saved his life. And Wellington relented. Even without an umbrella, he said, Tony Fortescue would look silly."

Philippa laughed as Lord Charles helped Clarissa down. "Sir Antony has never told me that story."

Lord Charles's face lit up as he turned to her. "Well, Tony's a shy chap. Doesn't like to boast."

"Of course," Philippa said with dancing eyes. "He wouldn't want it to get around town that the Duke had praised him so highly! I shall have to tell Sally Jersey, and Emily Cowper, and Lord Alvanley, perhaps."

Lord Charles grinned. "Tony'll shoot me. But I'll send on to you with my dying breath."

"You must tell me the beginning of the story, though, before I spread it around London. What exactly was he doing with the umbrella?"

"Can't he tell you later, Phil?" Clarissa entreated. "We want to talk to you. Just think, the Prince bowed to us! And we saw Mr. Byng, all dressed in green, in the Park! And we had two ices each!"

"Petits cochons!" Philippa said lovingly. "Thanks so much for taking them out, Lord Charles. I have a feeling in my bones they will speak of nothing else for a week!"

"Then you, like Tony Fortescue, will be wanting to shoot me!"

"Never, Lord Charles."

Philippa smiled up at him for a moment. He started to speak, but his horses suddenly pawed impatiently behind him. He leapt back up into his curricle and waved to the children. "Good-bye. I do hope, Miss Winslow, Robert there isn't ill. He had *three* ices! I shall see you soon."

Philippa, as she shepherded the chattering children back into the house, wondered what Lord Charles had been about to say to her. He, in truth, didn't know himself.

The silly story he had told reminded Lord Charles that he meant to ask Antony Fortescue to accompany him to a forthcoming fight in Richmond. Accordingly, he called at Sir Antony's chambers in Jermyn Street early the next afternoon. Tony's *bâtman* now valeted for him and was delighted to see Lord Charles again. After ten minutes, Lord Charles managed to extract from him that Sir Antony had planned to spend the afternoon at his club. Fifteen minutes later, Lord Charles strolled into White's.

The hour was early yet, but White's, as always, was filled with people. Lord Charles had ascertained from the doorman that Sir Antony had not yet arrived, so he walked quickly through the great center room, nodding to those of his acquaintance sitting there. He took the *Morning Chronicle* from the rosewood table littered with periodicals and settled in a capacious leather armchair, just beyond the imposing bay window that was White's most famous feature. He was soon absorbed in a review of the production of *Measure for Measure* at Covent Garden. This Mr. Hazlitt, Lord Charles noted with amusement, shared Philippa's dissatisfaction with Miss O'Neill's performance.

While Lord Charles was reading, the Marquis of Alvanley, a stout yet impeccably-clothed middle-aged gentleman, entered the club. He took his accustomed seat in the great bay window and raised his eyeglass at the passers-by. He was distracted from this agreeable occupation by his old friend, the wit Henry Luttrell, who greeted him heartily. Lord Charles, sitting nearby, could not but hear this interchange. He liked Mr. Luttrell very much indeed, but was barely acquainted with the Marquis, and decided forcing his company on the two of them would be improper. He returned to his newspaper and tried not to overhear their conversation. He succeeded for some time, but was roused abruptly when Lord Alvanley mentioned a name he knew.

"I hear the stakes are six to one Carlington will marry the Winslow girl," the Marquis drawled.

Lord Charles chuckled and, eager to hear more, shrank into his seat.

"She's a sweet girl," Mr. Luttrell replied. "Her dancing's *absolument exquis*. Not like an Englishwoman at all."

"It's a damn good match for her. Seems unfair to Carlington, though, when he don't know the full situation."

Lord Charles swore under his breath and wondered what on earth Alvanley was talking about.

"You mean Rupert?" Luttrell asked.

"Quite. Never liked that fellow, and, d'you know, I saw him yesterday in a waistcoat that was positively lavender! Not at all the thing."

"I hardly think, my dear Alvanley, her father's sartorial incompetence should prevent Miss Winslow from marrying well. There's more to it, isn't there?"

"How d'you know?"

"You only have to look at the man. He's finally losing a little of his infuriating insouciance. Must be something pretty bad for Rupert Winslow to be worried."

"I heard from Barrymore—although God knows Barrymore would say anything—that Winslow will be bankrupt by the end of the month. Others speak of it too. Wouldn't be so bad if the chit were married. Carlington could hush it up. All those Stauntons are as rich as Croesus. But if he hasn't come up to the mark yet, I shouldn't think he will at all. Scares one off a bit, having one's father-in-law in debt."

"Just a bit," Mr. Luttrell said drily. "But surely matters can't be that bad. They've a sizeable estate in Oxfordshire, haven't they?"

"Entailed," Lord Alvanley replied tersely.

"What about the London house? Sell it, and the family could move down to the country on a repairing lease. Cause talk, of course, but better than fleeing to the Continent to avoid the bailiffs."

"From what I hear, selling the house won't cover Winslow's debts. True profligate, y'know. Friend of

Cripplegate's. It'll be an open scandal, I fear. Close to that now."

"The poor gel!"

"Poor Carlington. Just when he's doing so well in the House, too. The Tories'll use it, that's certain. They could do a lot with it."

"That's true. Profligacy and sin in a great Whig family! Not only the Stauntons—Winslow's a connexion of the Duke of Hetford, ain't he? Be hard to hush it up even if Carlington were married to the chit already."

"Y'know," said Lord Alvanley seriously, "I think the Earl should be warned. He might marry her all the same—he certainly seems besotted—but he should know what kind of scandal-broth he's getting into."

"Can't one just drop a word in his ear?"

"Not the sort of thing one can just idly tell a chap. You'd have to know Carlington a dashed sight better than I do to interfere. I know Blawith well enough, but not his son. And Blawith, even if he weren't in America, couldn't deal with anything of this sort. He can't talk to anyone who doesn't have feathers. *You* don't know Carlington, I suppose?"

"Oh, no, Alvanley! You can't get me into this. I've never spoken to the Earl. Met his brother in Paris last autumn."

"That's it!"

Luttrell, who had presented this piece of information quite idly, was shocked by Alvanley's vehemence. "What's it?"

"You tell young Staunton. He's the proper person to inform Carlington."

Henry Luttrell didn't need to stop to think about the suggestion. "It won't do, my dear boy, it won't do."

"Why not?" Alvanley asked. "You could casually mention Sir Rupert's debts."

"I could not."

"Surely you know the chap well enough. Saw you with him at dinner here last week."

"Oh, I know him quite well. Charming young man."

"Well, then, what could be the objection? Seems very proper to me."

"It wouldn't work."

"Why not?" Alvanley impatiently demanded.

Mr. Luttrell was goaded by Alvanley's persistence. "Charles Staunton is in love with the Winslow chit himself, damn it! Anyone can see that!"

Lord Charles stood up. He threw down his paper and stalked between the two men, his face like thunder.

Mr. Luttrell was the first to move. He burst out laughing. "Now the fat's in the fire right enough! What do you suppose that scene meant? I wonder where he's going."

"I haven't the slightest idea," Lord Alvanley answered coldly.

Lord Charles did not know any more than did Lord Alvanley where he was going. He strode with a savage step down St. James's Street, oblivious to the calls of the fresh-faced young gentleman who had seen him leaving White's.

"Charles!" called the young man. "Charles, damn you, wait a minute!"

Lord Charles finally heard and, with an exasperated sigh, turned to greet Antony Fortescue.

"I say, Charles, you're just the man I'm looking for. There's a fight at Richmond a week from Friday. Just heard about it at Jackson's. The new African against Mendoza. Will you join me?"

"God, no, Antony! I've better things to do!" Lord Charles snapped. "Good day!"

He left behind him a considerably confused young man, whose bewilderment was not much abated when he entered White's and heard Mr. Luttrell's story.

Lord Charles himself could hardly think straight. He had had no idea Sir Rupert was in such desperate financial straits. Philippa would be ruined unless she married well. Philippa was set on marrying the Earl, and so she should. George would be miserable, caught up in an open scandal, but that didn't matter next to Philippa's happiness and security. Unless, of course, Lord Charles could persuade Philippa to marry him instead. Luttrell was right, of course, although Lord Charles had been blind to his own emotions. He loved Philippa, loved her more than Carlington, with his pettifogging speeches and ponderous affairs, ever could. She could never be happy with George, and he had been a fool to help the girl he loved marry another. Lord Charles turned exultantly toward Half Moon Street. He would tell Philippa, tell her that he loved her and that the thought of her as his brother's wife made his blood run cold.

Philippa sat with the tea-pot delicately poised in her hand.

"Lord Carlington," she said again, "may I pour you some more tea?"

The Earl turned away from the fireplace, whose elegant eighteenth-century mantel he had been raptly contemplating. Philippa did hope he hadn't noticed the large chip on the left side.

"More tea, Lord Carlington?" she asked for the third time.

"Er, no. No, thank you, Miss Winslow."

"Are you quite all right, Lord Carlington?" Philippa ventured. "You seem extraordinarily preoccupied."

The Earl started to apologise.

"No, no. I don't mind," Philippa assured him. "I'm sure you have weighty affairs on your mind."

"Yes, I do, Miss Winslow. There will be a vote in the next few days, I may tell you in confidence, on this Austrian question."

95

Philippa thought fleetingly that she couldn't imagine why the Earl thought a vote on so prosaic a matter as a new tariff agreement had to be kept secret, but she was quick to sympathise.

"No wonder you are preoccupied! What do you think will happen, Lord Carlington?"

"It would be improper for me to divulge any more specific information, ma'am—"

"Of course," Philippa dulcetly agreed.

"—than to tell you I am optimistic. Yes, I am optimistic," repeated Lord Carlington, warming to his theme.

"You feel the vote will go with you?"

"I don't know that I can go so far as to say that, but I can assure you, Miss Winslow, personally assure you that the Party will make a good showing."

"How gratifying!" Philippa murmured.

"Yes, indeed. I must say, Miss Winslow, that this subject has been a pressing concern of mine for years. Metternich clearly rules Austria, and it is essential to our national safety not to anger the Prince by any rash acts. There are those, however—"

Philippa saw that the Earl was launching on one of his lengthy monologues and found it impossible to pay any very close attention to what he was saying. She smiled sweetly at him while he spoke on and on. She wondered if she had done right to engage the new housemaid. The expense might be a problem, but she would have to ask her father. He hadn't gone to Hoare's to withdraw money for her for the household expenses yet this month; she would have to remind him. They did need another servant, if only to accompany Isabella around town. She was too old to go out by herself any more. Philippa was just wondering if Isabella had remembered to return those books to Hookham's, when Lord Carlington abruptly stopped in his speech, which, even for him, had been inordinately long.

"I beg your pardon, Miss Winslow," he said. "I had forgotten that you, of course, can have no interest in foreign affairs."

Philippa thought ruefully that she *was* interested, just not in Lord Carlington's view of them, but she muttered a polite disclaimer. Lord Carlington nodded perfunctorily.

"You see, Miss Winslow, I did not come here today to tell you this. I . . . er, I want to . . . I plan . . ."

"Yes?" Philippa demurely inquired.

"What I mean to say is . . . is that I have in the past weeks grown to admire and respect you more than any other woman I know. Would you do me the inestimable honour, Miss Winslow, of accepting my hand in marriage?"

Philippa had not expected this so soon. Nor would she have thought that the Earl of Carlington, that rising young orator, would have had such difficulty framing a simple question. He'd done very well, precisely obeying all the manuals, once he had gotten started, but she was surprised that he seemed even slightly unsure of himself. He knew his worth, and all London could have told him what her answer would be. Even more to her surprise, she herself stumbled in her reply.

"Lord Carlington, I . . . I am grateful . . . and honoured." She thought with irritation that this sounded as if she meant to refuse him and hastily said: "I shall be most happy to become your wife."

Lord Carlington embraced her chastely, planting a kiss on her cheek.

"I shall of course have to ask your father's permission to our betrothal, but I shouldn't think he will object."

"No," Philippa quite sincerely agreed. "He will be delighted at the prospect."

"Shall we be married in June?"

"That would be lovely."

"St. George's, Hanover Square, of course?"

"Of course."

"I shall send a notice to the *Gazette* as soon as I obtain your father's consent."

"I see I can rely on you, my lord, to arrange everything."

"From now on, my dear Philippa."

Philippa smiled meekly, and Lord Carlington took his leave. His look of cheerful satisfaction immediately informed Jarvis of what had taken place. Lord Charles, however, was far too occupied with his own thoughts when he met his brother on the doorstep to draw the same conclusion. Indeed, embarrassed at meeting him, he barely glanced at the Earl.

"Oh, hullo, George. I was just going to see Miss Winslow myself. Promised to take her to the theatre next week, you know."

Lord Charles tried to slip past the Earl into the house, but Carlington jovially buttonholed him.

"You can't go, Charles. I have a piece of news for you. I think—I know—you will be pleased to hear Miss Winslow has agreed to marry me!"

"Oh. Just now?" Lord Charles asked with a curious blank look on his face.

"Yes, five minutes ago! I am the happiest man alive."

"Philippa's going to marry you," Lord Charles said as if to impress it on his mind. "She's a lovely girl, George."

"I told you weeks ago you would like her!" The Earl slapped his brother on the back. "I must go tell Mother."

"Yes. Do that," Lord Charles slowly said. "Tell me, George, what would you think of a novel portraying the Regent as a villain, a sinister Italian, say?"

"Why . . . I suppose I would think a dashed piece of insolence. Libellous, too! But why d'you ask?"

"Never mind. It isn't important." Lord Charles smiled wanly and walked away.

That evening Philippa Winslow was unusually gay. Her family took her news well. Robin politely grumbled that anyone who had given him such a stuffy book wasn't likely to be the best new brother, but Henry Francis warmly wished Philippa all happiness.

"Just think, you'll be a *Countess!*" Isabella sighed. "And when his father dies, you'll be a Marchioness! With ermine robes and strawberry leaves and everything."

"Strawberry leaves are on a Duke's coronet, not a Marquis's," Philippa informed her. "And can you imagine Lord Carlington in ermine? I can't. But you're right, sweetheart. It *will* be nice."

"Can I carry flowers for you at the wedding?" Clarissa wanted to know. "And will I have a new frock for it?"

"Of course you will. Just like me. What do you think I should wear?"

The girls spent dinner, much to Robin's disgust, discussing Philippa's wedding gown. After dinner Philippa excused herself and retired to her room. She locked the door and irrationally burst into hysterical tears. She was happy, she assured herself, gloriously happy. She had succeeded and she and the children were provided for for the rest of their lives. Her betrothal would be formally announced in a few days, as soon as her father, who had not shown up for dinner, could be found. She could want no more in the world. Still she cried, late into the night, without being able to supply herself with the slightest reason for her misery.

Lord Charles Staunton was also up late that night. He sat in a club, a noisy place, far from St. James's Street and White's. Despite the solicitations he received, Lord Charles remained alone in a corner. He drank steadily until he could no longer remember what it was he was trying to forget.

Lord Carlington sat up in his study, a map of Europe before him.

"Two weeks in Paris, and then a month in Italy. It will be hot in July, so three days, say, in Rome, and then the seaside. I must tell Philippa."

The Earl of Carlington put away his map and contentedly retired to bed.

Chapter Ten

When Lord Carlington tracked Sir Rupert to earth two days later, Sir Rupert not only gave his wholehearted blessing to the match, but also reminded Lord Carlington of the little card-party the Earl had so reluctantly agreed to attend.

"Tomorrow night, Carlington! Bring your brother! Be a real family party now, eh what? Come to dinner, too. Must get acquainted, y'know, must get acquainted."

Lord Carlington in turn reminded his brother. Lord Charles swore and said he'd cry off.

"I don't want to be there while you have a quiet dinner with your betrothed," he said quite sincerely. "*De trop* and all that."

"Charles," the Earl severely replied, "if you remember, you accepted this invitation. I didn't even want to attend. I still don't. Card-parties, y'know. Not at all my forte."

All Lord Charles could say was that things had

changed since the invitation was issued. "You weren't betrothed to Miss Winslow then."

"All the more reason for you to attend. Can't go around insulting your new relations, Charles! I don't think you've even spoken to Philippa since I told you the news. You must do the pretty and felicitate her. She's so fond of you."

Lord Charles winced. Yet he would have to accustom himself to seeing Philippa and George together; "Very well," he sighed. "I will be there."

Despite this gracious concession, and Lord Carlington's happy mood, the dinner was not a success. Henry Francis, who had spent the day with his father's bankers, was deeply worried. Sir Rupert might airily inform him that there was nothing to worry about now that Philippa had snared a peer, and one with the wealth of a nabob, but Henry Francis thought this a specious argument. Carlington would pay off Sir Rupert's debts, no doubt, if Sir Rupert did indeed go bankrupt, but not only was that distasteful to Henry Francis, it also would hardly stop a scandal from spreading. Only if the Earl dealt with Sir Rupert's creditors before they went to law could it be kept quiet, and even Sir Rupert balked at asking his future son-in-law for a thousand or so pounds within a week of his daughter's engagement. Henry Francis had tried to present this problem to his father, but Sir Rupert merely laughed and said it could all be dealt with.

As he watched his guests eat the excellent curry of rabbits Philippa had ordered, Sir Rupert decided that one way of staving off disaster would be to win at cards tonight. Both Stauntons would have money on them—quite enough, if he won heavily, to get him through this week. And Sir Rupert could always win heavily when he set his mind to it. He was almost as cheerful as Carlington during dinner. Carlington was beaming proprietorily on Philippa, setting Lord Charles's teeth on edge. Philippa herself didn't enjoy it very much. She felt curiously languid, as she had since accepting the Earl's proposal, and she hardly spoke. Lord Charles was also unusually silent. The curry of rabbits, saddle of mutton, and mulligatawny soup might as well have been paper from the way he ate them, Philippa thought. The only thing he paid any heed to was the wine, which he imbibed with some show of enthusiasm. The conversation faltered often, with only Sir Rupert and Lord Carlington speaking.

"I think we shall go to Paris," Lord Carlington said. "I've never been there, but my mother tells me it's a fine city."

Sir Rupert gulped a little at this. "Your generation has been deprived, my dear Earl. Paris is not a fine city." He helped himself to more wine. "Paris, my dear boy, is quite simply the center of the world."

"I beg your pardon?" Lord Carlington said, bridling. "Surely you, an Englishman, can't believe that?"

"I tell you, Paris is the center of civilization. The best wine, the best food, the best women—all there!"

Lord Carlington did not approve of this statement at all, as well as thinking it remarkably improper before Philippa. "I have always been glad," he painstakingly explained, "that the disturbances on the Continent prevented my travel abroad. It is my profound conviction that one must know one's country inside and out before venturing abroad. Particularly when one, like myself, plans to work at Westminster for the good of the entire nation. I have visited every city of any importance in England. There is far more, sir, to be learned from recent developments in Liverpool or Manchester than in Paris or Vienna."

"Do you know Liverpool and Manchester well, Lord Carlington?" Henry Francis asked. The Earl was delighted with the question.

"I know them better, I assure you, Mr. Winslow,

than any other man of my station. I visit these new 'factory' towns frequently. Indeed, I plan to maintain residence in some such town for several months of each year. It should be extremely interesting, not to say inspiring, to watch our nation's industrial classes."

"My God!" Lord Charles muttered in disgust to Henry Francis. "I wouldn't want to sit back and watch the grass grow, like you, but it's certainly preferable to watching treadmills whirl!"

Philippa too was dismayed. "Really?" she said hesitantly. "Manchester?"

Lord Carlington smiled at her. "I'm sure you'll enjoy it, my dear. There are many worthy charitable organizations for the relief of the unfortunate in these northern towns that will welcome the aid and patronage of the Countess of Carlington."

"What an inducement!" Lord Charles muttered again to Henry Francis.

Philippa gave the Earl a little forced smile. "How charming."

"Sounds deadly dull to me," Sir Rupert said with devastating frankness.

Since Lord Carlington was obviously preparing to attempt to disabuse Sir Rupert of this misapprehension, Philippa gratefully realised she could at last leave the gentlemen to their port. She retired to her bedroom rather than the drawing-room, pleading a headache. As she mounted the stairs, she could hear the Earl patiently saying to her father: "Not at all sir. Why, Manchester even has its own Historical Museum and Antiquarian Society."

The rest of the party could not escape, and they were forced to hear the beauties and cultural advantages of Manchester enumerated for well over an hour. At last Sir Rupert suggested to Lord Carlington that the evening really had been planned as a card-party.

"Ah, but that would be rather tedious, don't you

think?" the Earl replied. "I'd be quite content just to talk here."

Even Henry Francis, who was usually bored by cards, protested at this, and Sir Rupert managed to bear them all off to the saloon in the rear of the house. He gave into Lord Carlington so much as to agree they play quadrille, usually a calm game. The Earl looked forward to an hour or two of placid boredom. Carlington was to be placidly bored, but for far more than an hour, and the atmosphere in the room was not really very calm at all.

They were still playing some four hours later. The stakes had been pushed extremely high, too high for Henry Francis, who had excused himself, but stayed up to keep an eye on his father. Carlington played his cards deliberately, carefully, taking no risks; he was losing badly. Sir Rupert and Lord Charles were superb players. Consummate gamblers, they took insane risks that, to Carlington's irritation, made them win time after time.

Lord Charles was playing with a passionate fervour, determined to think of nothing but his cards. A slight glitter in his eye revealed how heavily he had been drinking, but his speech was clear and his playing, as always, was brilliant.

Sir Rupert was playing with an assumed nonchalance. He leaned back in his chair and idly gossiped, trying to look at ease, but no one—except perhaps the Earl—was deceived. His cravat was twisted, his hair dishevelled, and his words slurred. Both he and Lord Charles seemed oblivious to their surroundings, fancying themselves perhaps in Watier's, or Crockford's, or some even less reputable gambling den.

Henry Francis wondered what was eating at Charles Staunton. He looked furiously angry or terribly worried: pale and with his jaw set. Noting the ferocity with which he was playing, Henry Francis decided that Lord Charles, despite the legendary Staunton wealth, might well be dangerously in debt.

Henry Francis, tired and restless, glanced round the room. It was stale and reeked of the cigars he and Lord Carlington had been smoking. There were empty wine bottles on the sideboards, and, Henry Francis fastidiously saw, claret had been spilled on the carpet. Ashes had been carelessly flicked onto the floor; wax had long since overrun the candlesticks on the mantelpiece and the table, coagulating into nasty pools. Even as Henry Francis looked, a candle guttered and went out. The fire too was almost dead; only a few smouldering embers remained. Nevertheless, Lord Carlington saw something that caught his attention, and held it. Then he spoke, and his severe voice echoed oddly in the dim room.

"I regret to inform you of this, Sir Rupert, but this card has been marked."

That jolted even Lord Charles. Everyone leapt to his feet. An uneasy silence fell. One of them had been cheating. Henry Francis was the first to speak.

"Let me look at that, Carlington," he savagely demanded. Carlington mutely held the ace out to him. Henry Francis snatched it from the Earl and, picking up a candelabrum, scanned its back meticulously. At last he sighed and put the card down.

"You're right, Carlington."

At once they all started to speak, babbling to hide their embarrassment. Sir Rupert finally silenced the others.

"Be quiet, all of you," he said with startling authority. "We did not open this deck."

"What does that matter?" Lord Charles said impatiently. "An X isn't scratched on a card unless someone has been cheating. One of us!"

"Not if it wasn't a new deck," Henry Francis said almost pleadingly. "Someone else could have done it."

"How many people play cards in your home, Winslow?" Lord Charles asked. "I don't think Sir Rupert gives a gaming-party here very often. He usually attends some, er, professional establishment. This evening was an exception, merely to spend time with his future son-in-law. Isn't that right, Sir Rupert?"

"Yes, yes, I suppose so," Sir Rupert said in a choked voice. Such a thing had never happened to him before. He had never been caught. He must be growing old.

"Unless you intend to blame your sister Philippa, or a footman," Lord Charles said silkily, "it must have been one of us, mustn't it? I wonder who."

"Charles, footmen don't play cards. At least, not in the house of their employment. And I refuse to believe Philippa had anything to do with this deplorable incident!" the Earl unnecessarily protested.

"I don't think your brother was seriously suggesting anything of the kind," Henry Francis kindly told him.

Lord Carlington's slightly protuberant eyes positively bulged.

"That means one of the four of us cheated at cards! Quite incredible!"

"What other solution is there, George?" Lord Charles wearily asked. "Unless you plan to blame young Robin. Or Clarissa."

"That's it! Young Robin must have done it. Hardly the act of a female. How distressing!"

"Oh, honestly, George! You can't be serious."

"It's the only acceptable solution."

"Not if it doesn't happen to be true!"

Henry Francis remained uncomfortably silent, horridly certain he knew the real culprit. Sir Rupert, though, had regained composure and assured Lord Carlington he must be correct.

"My young scapegrace must have tampered with it!

Winning money off his innocent sisters, I daresay. How he'll be punished."

"You know, Miss Winslow will hear of this unpleasant discovery if you punish the boy, Sir Rupert. I can't imagine you'd like that, George," Lord Charles quietly pointed out. He spoke softly to Henry Francis: "She'd never believe it, you know. Which might be awkward. Don't let your father scold Robin."

Henry Francis nodded, surprised at Lord Charles's concern.

The Earl was loudly explaining that, regardless of the wound to Miss Winslow, justice must be served at all costs. Young Robin must be properly chastised. Sir Rupert, on the other hand, was in perfect agreement with Lord Charles that this must be hushed up as far as possible. Philippa was a discerning girl and would never believe Robin had cheated at cards. That could prove quite unpleasant. And Robin, if punished for something he didn't do, would be sure to tell Philippa. No, despite the Earl of Carlington's tirades, Sir Rupert hadn't the slightest intention of whipping his son. Sir Rupert assured Lord Carlington, however, that justice would be done. The Earl was pacified and said he was sure he could rely on Sir Rupert's paternal authority to root out his son's depraved tendencies.

Henry Francis went quietly round the room, extinguishing some of the guttering candles. The fire was now completely burned out. The party was clearly over. Lord Charles, shaken into sobriety by the ugly scene, nudged his brother and hinted they ought to be leaving. The Earl, extremely sleepy, was only too glad to hear this. Henry Francis woke the footman asleep in the hall and sent him to gather the visitors' coats. They had tacitly agreed to close the question of the marked card; Robin Winslow was a convenient culprit. The matter could be forgotten now, and everyone but the Earl breathed deeply, realising that. Lord Carlington and his brother retrieved their coats and thanked the Winslows for a most enjoyable evening. Then they heard a cry from upstairs.

"Help!" Robin called. "Henry Francis, is that you? Please help! My candle's blown out and I can't see."

"God damn it," Lord Charles said through his teeth, hoping the Earl wouldn't make a fool of himself.

Henry Francis flashed Lord Charles a sympathetic glance.

"I'll go up and put him back to bed, Father. God knows what he's doing," he quickly said.

"But don't you think this is a most opportune moment to scold the little rascal, Sir Rupert? Shouldn't leave for tomorrow what you can do today, and all that."

"I don't intend to give my son a hiding in the middle of the night, Lord Carlington," Sir Rupert said.

"No, no. But you should tell him he's been caught in his wickedness. He's fond of me, I know. Perhaps it would make an impression if I said something," the Earl replied.

"I think we should go home, George. Robin's bad behaviour isn't any of our business," Lord Charles firmly said.

"Not your business, Charles, but it's certainly mine. The lad will live with Philippa and me, for a while at least, and it wouldn't suit me at all to give shelter to a dishonest child." The Earl lowered his voice. "And I don't trust Winslow. He's to blame, you know. Hasn't brought his son up properly. In this case, I feel it's my duty to see the boy is made aware of the awesome nature of his crime."

Ignoring his brother's restraining hand on his sleeve and the indignant expostulations of both Winslows, Lord Carlington walked over to the stairway.

"Come down here at once, Robert!" he called up.

Robin replied, with justifiable exasperation, "My candle's blown out! I can't see! I want Henry Francis."

"I'll go up to him," Henry Francis said, stepping toward the stairs.

"Don't bother, Winslow. I'll bring him down," said the Earl.

He walked up to the landing, carrying a candle from the hall table with him, took the hapless boy by the ear, and sternly propelled him down the stairs.

When they reached the others, Henry Francis said through his teeth: "Kindly take your hands off my brother, my Lord."

Carlington obeyed but had clearly not abandoned his crusade to lead Robin back to the path of righteousness.

"My boy," he thundered, "you have done a wicked thing!"

Henry Francis interrupted him. "What are you doing out of bed, Robin?" he asked calmly.

"My tooth hurts. Horribly! I thought I could get some laudanum drops without waking anyone."

"Yes, that was kind of you. Philippa's been very tired lately. And one should never disturb the servants. I'll take you to the storeroom. You understand, Lord Carlington. If the boy's in pain, that must be dealt with before anything else."

Henry Francis made the sketchiest of bows and took his brother's hand. Unfortunately, Robin caught sight of Lord Charles. Lord Charles was frowning harshly, and Robin suddenly realised that, in front of a real soldier, it was childish to make a fuss about an aching tooth.

"Oh, I'm not in pain, Henry. I can bear it perfectly easily. It's not as if I were wounded."

Lord Charles grinned and winked at Robin.

The Earl stepped forward again. "Well, then, Robin,

if you are not in pain, you can hear what I have to say to you."

"Not now, George! For God's sake!" Lord Charles angrily exclaimed.

Lord Carlington paid him no heed and said very kindly to Robin, "I was shocked, my lad, and grieved, to learn of your behaviour."

Robin blinked under this unexpected attack, mentally reviewing his recent transgressions, but bore it nobly.

"I am sorry to hear that, Lord Carlington."

His flat statement sounded impudent, and the Earl was incensed.

"A boy who does not scruple to steal—for I put it no higher—" the Earl told him, "can have nothing but a life of shame before him."

"But . . . I never . . . I mean . . ." Robin stammered in astonishment.

"Marking a card is the act of a cad, Robin. It is dishonourable in the extreme. You must be a great sorrow to your family."

Robin was sleepy and confused. Lord Carlington's resounding and mysterious words might have reduced him to tears had Lord Charles not winked at him again. Robin was not going to lower himself by pleas or vulgar denials when Captain Lord Charles Staunton was watching him.

"Yes, sir. I am sorry, sir. Cheating at cards is a very wicked thing."

Lord Charles sighed in relief. Any strenuous denials from Robin might have made even Carlington think again. Henry Francis took Robin off to forage in the storeroom, and Lord Carlington put his hand fraternally on Sir Rupert's shoulder.

"So sorry about all this, Winslow. Terribly sad to see a child gone to the bad like that. And Philippa's so

111

fond of him. It hurts to think of such a promising lad gone astray."

"Oh, God!" Lord Charles exclaimed in acute distaste. "I suppose your having endowed him with Locke's *Treatises* makes it all the worse!"

"Exactly," Lord Carlington said amiably.

With that, Lord Charles was finally able to push his brother out of the house. He wished Sir Rupert a hasty good night.

"And I recommend you grease your footman's fist," he called back from the doorstep. "Damned interesting scene, this was."

The footman, sitting unobtrusively in the corner of the hall, blushed. Sir Rupert laughed and pressed a half-guinea into the boy's hand.

"You don't remember, d'you, my lad? Now off to bed."

Sir Rupert's pockets jingled as he walked back to the saloon and snuffed out the two last candles glittering there. Then he extinguished the one Carlington had set back down on the hall table. His luck had held after all. He was two hundred pounds wealthier, and no one would say a thing about that distressing mark on the back of the ace of hearts. Lord Charles was right enough, he thought; it was a pity Philippa would hear of this episode. It didn't matter, though. Even if she suspected the truth, she would hardly tell anyone her father was a cheat. No, he was safe—and he had money in his pockets. Sir Rupert went to bed well pleased with himself.

Chapter Eleven

~~~~~~

Philippa always rose early, but the next morning even she felt Robin woke her at an unreasonable hour. Ignoring Petherton's flurried admonitions, he stormed into Philippa's bedroom at half-past six. He stood by the head of her bed, glaring down at his sister.

"I want you to wake up!"

Philippa yawned. She sat up and shook her curls out of her face.

"I should hope you do," she said. "I mean, if you *didn't* want me to wake up, you'd be going about it quite the wrong way."

Robin ignored this pleasantry and sat down heavily on the side of the bed.

"I have to talk to you!"

"Has Clarissa hidden your box of tin soldiers again? Or has Isabella refused to take you to the Park? I'm sure your terrible grievance can wait till breakfast. Let me sleep!"

Philippa curled up again, turning her back to her brother. Robin prodded her.

"You don't understand! It's something much, much worse! It's that odious Earl of yours!"

Philippa did not move.

"He's not my Earl," she mumbled. "That is, he is, but it's not a proper way to refer to him."

"I don't care! You mustn't marry him! He insulted me!"

Philippa was still unimpressed, but she did sit up.

"What's Carlington done, except giving you that ill-judged *cadeau?*" she asked reasonably.

"He's . . . he's maligned me!" Robin said.

"Robin, what *are* you talking about?"

Robin poured forth the story of his wrongs, just as Lord Charles had feared, into his sister's attentive ear.

"Carlington said you'd cheated at cards with your sister?" Philippa demanded incredulously. "He must have been foxed! What a ridiculous statement! What was he thinking of?"

"I truly don't know. Clarissa cheats sometimes, but she wouldn't ever mark a card!"

"Mark cards!" Philippa exclaimed. "Is that what they were talking about?"

"I just told you that!"

"Good Lord, how appalling! Even if Carlington were in his cups—*someone* must have marked the card." Philippa had forgotten her brother's presence.

"One of the men last night must have cheated, isn't that what it means, Philippa?"

"Not at all, Robin! There are lots of other solutions! But I know you didn't do it, don't worry. Lord Carlington must simply have had too much to drink. That's not a reason not to marry him! Now go away and let me get dressed!"

Philippa sprang out of bed as soon as Robin left the room. She didn't bother ringing for hot water, but poured

cold water from the jug directly into the basin. She
splashed the water onto her face, directing Petherton over
her shoulder to select a dress for her. She stepped into the
underthings and frock Petherton had laid out and threaded
a ribbon through her curls, pulling them severely away
from her face. Henry Francis prided himself on keeping
country hours, even in town, and Philippa hoped he
would be awake. A gentle knock at his door elicited no
answer, however, and Philippa, remembering that he must
have had a late night, contented herself with descending
to the servants' hall and asking his valet to inform her
brother when he arose that she wished to speak to him at
the earliest opportunity. She thought of leaving a similar
message for Sir Rupert, but decided he was unlikely to
obey such a summons, and she would not get much information out of him if he did. In any case, Sir Rupert
never rose before one.

Philippa was far too distraught to return to bed. She
sipped at a cup of coffee, but was unable to eat more than
a muffin. She picked up Walter Scott's latest novel. She
was fond of Scott, but today she could not keep her mind
on the adventures of the tragic Claverhouse or even charming Jenny Dennison and threw down *Old Mortality* after
half an hour. If she were going to be miserable and restless all morning, she decided, she might as well do something profitable. She rang for Jarvis and asked him to
bring up the month's accounts. Philippa hated doing accounts. They seemed an appropriate way to occupy her
tortured morning. To think that any one of those four, of
each of whom she was so fond, could have stooped so low
as to cheat at a private card-party cut her to the quick.

The household accounts proved, if not absorbing, at
least time-consuming, and it was close on noon when
Philippa emerged from the study, blinking, tired of figures
of all denominations. They had, as usual, barely enough
money to cover their expenses. Philippa sighed as she
realised she could not after all buy that shawl of Norwich

silk she had so admired in a Bond Street window; Clarissa's new boots would have to come out of her sister's pocket-money.

She rang again for Henry Francis's valet. Satterthwaite was most apologetic: "I did tell him, ma'am, but he apparently did not, er, apprehend the urgency of your request. Mr. Winslow left at eleven. He said he would see you when he returned."

"Where did he go?" Philippa asked fiercely.

"I believe, ma'am, Mr. Winslow intended to pay a call on the Earl of Carlington."

"Oh, indeed," Philippa muttered. "What *is* going on?"

She thanked Satterthwaite and, taking a footman with her, set off for Blawith House.

Her elder brother was having a reassuring morning. He had called on the Stauntons to apologise for the unpleasant incident and to ensure that neither of them intended to spread the story about. His father had cheated, Henry Francis was sure of that. The others must have guessed it easily enough. If they were willing to keep quiet, to accept the cock-and-bull story that Robin was responsible, then Philippa could marry her Earl and all would be well. Sir Rupert might—indeed, surely would—continue to cheat, but, if Philippa were the Countess of Carlington, whatever scandals might break later, the family would not starve.

Henry Francis found the Stauntons perfectly amenable to his suggestions that this story not be repeated. Lord Charles met his apology with a bland smile.

"But since your brother was of course responsible for the sorry affair, my dear Winslow, you hardly need to concern yourself with an apology. I quite understand how it came to pass. And naturally you don't want the story repeated. As my brother would say, it's sad to think of such a promising lad gone astray."

Henry Francis was not deceived by Lord Charles's solemnity.

"Yes, we're planning to ship Robin off to Australia," he said mildly.

Lord Charles laughed and sent Henry Francis up to his brother's dressing-room.

"George is still tying his cravat. He'll be an age about it. Just go up. He won't mind the interruption."

Lord Carlington was even more reassuring than his brother had been. The Earl seemed wholeheartedly to accept Robin's guilt. It seemed incredible he did not suspect Sir Rupert, but Henry Francis concluded the Earl simply could not, once he had derived one solution, conceive of any other. Lord Charles was right; the Earl did not mind the interruption at all. He insisted Henry Franics sit down and advise him on his neckcloth.

"The Mathematical, do you think, Winslow? Or a simpler style?

Henry Francis cared little for the proper tying of neckcloths and adroitly turned the conversation to politics. He and the Earl were still discussing the possible—and, to a Whig, deplorable—entrance of the Duke of Wellington into politics when Philippa arrived at Blawith House.

"I'm sorry, Miss. Lord Carlington and a gentleman caller are upstairs. Perhaps you could wait?"

Philippa couldn't very well ask to be shown up to the Earl's dressing-room. She was desperate to talk to someone, though, and asked if Lord Charles were at home.

"Indeed he is, Miss. In the morning room."

"Give him this card, please."

Lord Charles rose to his feet with an oath when he read Philippa's scrawled words of entreaty. Lord Charles knew Sir Rupert had cheated. To blame anyone else was laughable. Philippa had doubtless come because she had heard the story and she must also have guessed her father was to blame. Lord Charles could imagine what that would mean to her. She could have few illusions left about her father, but she must be dreadfully ashamed. She must have come to Carlington House, like her brother, to find out if he and George intended to tell the world of Sir Rupert's conduct. Her future was at stake, the betrothal Philippa had fought so hard for might be broken. He could reassure her easily enough, but the prospect of a *tête-à-tête* with her was unwelcome. She cared nothing for him; she was to marry his brother. Why should he have to tell her father was safe because George was a fool? Henry Francis, or Carlington himself, should give her the good news. He rang for the butler, intending to send Miss Winslow upstairs.

Then Lord Charles glanced again at Philippa's card, where she had scrawled merely: "I must see you. Please." His eyes softened. He was going to leave England and in- spect the family estates in Antigua, he decided. Perhaps after that he'd visit his father in Brazil. He couldn't bear acting as best man at Philippa's wedding; he didn't want to see the happy couple. His mother would be disturbed at his abrupt departure, but then, she had never expected him to settle down into society with ease. He would tell her he had found it impossible to live in London. He would not return to England. And he deserved a final meeting with Philippa. He could carry its memory with him across the sea. She was his friend as well as his beloved, and she was in trouble.

"Show Miss Winslow in," he instructed the butler.

Lord Charles carefully pulled the panelled doors to behind her. She was very pale, in a white dress without ornamentation. She took off her simple chip hat and sat down on one of the delicate Hepplewhite chairs facing the fireplace. She was silent for a moment, twisting the ribbons of her hat between her fingers. Lord Charles crossed the room to face her. He leaned against the green marble mantel, throwing his arm along it so that the Sèvres fig- urines his mother had painstakingly chosen some thirty years before shook ominously.

"Yes, Miss Winslow?" he drawled.

"Lord Charles," Philippa said, her eyes on the bonnet in her lap, "could you please . . . could you have the goodness to tell me what . . . exactly what happened at my house last night?"

"Don't you feel, Miss Winslow, that that question might better be addressed to your brother or your affianced husband?"

Philippa raised her eyes to him. "You're my friend," she said quietly.

Lord Charles stiffly recounted the bare story of Carlington's discovery. At the end of his tale, Philippa, who had been listening with a set, taut expression, shuddered and covered her face with her hands. After a moment she looked up again, shaking slightly.

"Dear God, you know, Lord Charles, this means I can't marry your brother."

Lord Charles winced at her obvious distress. It was tempting to gather her into his arms and tell her to marry him instead, but he knew that would not help Philippa. He could imagine her indignation. She wanted to marry Carlington; she had made that clear enough. She might even love Carlington, in some cool, detached way. Declaring his own love could only hurt Philippa; she would have lost a friend.

"I hardly see that, my dear," he answered her calmly. "Just because your little brother is guilty of ungentlemanly conduct doesn't mean Carlington will break your engagement. Although you may have the greatest difficulty persuading him Robin isn't a dyed-in-the-wool reprobate!"

"Oh, stop it! Carlington's far too courteous to ask to be released from our agreement, but do you think I could marry him with the threat of a scandal like that hanging over me? I can't ruin all his political ambitions! You know as well as I, Lord Charles, that it's not my brother's conduct I blush for!"

Philippa turned away from him. Tears rolled down

her cheeks as she stared blankly out the grand French window. Lord Charles could not bear to see her in such agony. He had no right to comfort her; watched miserably as she bit her lip and tried to control her tears. He thought of getting Carlington, but then realised that could only make things worse. Philippa felt honour-bound to break her engagement, now that she had discovered her father's shameful behaviour; she would hardly look for comfort in her betrothed's arms. Lord Charles could think of only one way to ease her situation. That way would lose him her friendship forever, but it would let her marry the man she had chosen. Lord Charles didn't want her friendship any longer. He wanted her love, and he couldn't have it. So he took that way.

"Miss Winslow, spare me your tears," he said harshly. "I have not yet told you the full story."

She looked at him. "What now?" she savagely asked.

"I did not tell you it all, Miss Winslow," Lord Charles declared in a clear, steely voice. "I did not tell you that I was the man who marked the card."

Philippa rose to her feet in one swift move.

"You!" she cried. "I can't believe it!"

Lord Charles was ridiculously pleased by this tribute and his voice shook slightly as he assured her that it was nevertheless quite true.

"Why?" she asked, taking a step away from him.

"We are not all as wealthy as my brother, Miss Winslow."

Philippa stood still for a moment, once again looking away. Lord Charles saw with a pang that she was absorbing this news, revising her opinion of him forever more. As he expected, anger was her next reaction. She whirled around and took a step toward him.

"How dare you? How dare you stand there and tell me to my face you cheated at cards? At a private party! In my house! I—" and her voice broke suddenly. "I wouldn't have thought it of you, Lord Charles."

"This can be a lesson to you, Miss Winslow, that people are not commonly either kind or virtuous, and that you yourself are not so worldly-wise as you like to think."

Philippa was stung by this. She murmured in stricken tones: "I trusted you. I was ready to condemn my own father before you. I knew you were a gambler. I knew you were reckless. Yet I trusted you."

"Your faith, I am afraid, was quite misplaced," Lord Charles replied coldly.

"Why do you tell me this? Don't you fear I'll have you publicly excoriated as the cad that you are?"

Lord Charles had thought of this. "I hardly think you'll do that, my dear. Carlington's political career would be blighted, you thought, if it were known that your father cheated at cards. Just think how much worse it would be for poor George if it were his own brother who'd done such a thing. His dearest companion and most trusted friend! No, I'm afraid you could never be a great political hostess then. Poor dear George would have to give up all hopes of the Cabinet. You wouldn't want that to happen, surely?"

"You disgust me! You gauged the situation precisely enough! I won't ever dare expose you, you're right! I'll degrade myself and protect your filthy secret! I shan't even tell Carlington—his heart would break! No, you wouldn't have told me if you hadn't known you could buy my silence. But why did you tell me?"

Lord Charles walked away from her to the window. Looking out on Grosvenor Street, he said with perfect honesty: "I am not a total scoundrel, Miss Winslow. I could not bear to see you condemn your father and break your engagement because of some mistaken sense of honour."

"I see," she slowly said. "You don't mind that my brother, never suspecting you, blames his own father. That your brother, who has never stooped to anything shameful in his life, thinks you the most trustworthy and honourable of men. I would have preferred you to be a total scoundrel, Lord Charles. Then I would not know what a fool I've been. Good day. I only wish we could never meet again."

She did not wait for Lord Charles to open the doors for her, but wrestled with them herself, leaving the room without deigning to glance at him again. Without waiting to see Henry Francis or Lord Carlington, she called her footman to her and almost ran out the door. Henry Francis, just leaving the Earl's dressing-room, caught sight of her hurrying down Grosvenor Street. He declined to make himself ridiculous by running after her, and he let her go on alone. When she reached Half Moon Street, Philippa locked herself in her room and sobbed for several minutes. But she decided very soon she could not permit herself the luxury of tears. She splashed cold water on her face and went up to the school-room to introduce Clarissa to the basic principles of the division of three-digit numbers.

Lord Charles also let himself out of the house without speaking to anyone. Telling the lie had been more painful even than he had expected. He went for a long walk along the Thames. He wore no hat and threw back his coat, revelling in the high wind as if it could blow away the memory of Philippa, of Philippa looking at him with utter contempt, telling him he disgusted her. The wind didn't blow it away, and he knew, as he returned slowly home many hours later, that he would never forget Philippa's scornful face.

Chapter Twelve

Years afterward Philippa could never remember what she had done between Lord Charles's awful disclosure and the ball at Almack's a week later. No doubt the week had been like any other; she had surely ridden in the Park, received callers, attended a dance or two, and courteously accepted felicitations as her betrothal became known. But she moved through it all in a daze, hardly aware of Lord Carlington's proprietary attentions or her family's anxious glances.

"Is Philippa quite well?" Isabella asked Henry Francis. "She's been so quiet lately."

"She ought to be *radiant*," Clarissa said knowledgeably. "That's what betrothed ladies in stories always are."

"Clarissa, you must learn not to expect life to resemble a romance. Philippa is certainly happy at her engagement. She may be a little tired," Henry Francis told the children.

"She forgot to take me out yesterday, when she promised!"

"Oh, Robin, Philippa's busy now, planning her wedding. You can hardly blame her for forgetting a casual appointment with her little brother."

"It wasn't casual, Henry. She promised!"

"And she *hasn't* been planning her wedding," Clarissa added. "Lord Carlington asked her if she would prefer the second week in June to the third and she said she didn't want to think about it yet."

"The Earl did not like that at all," Robin contributed. "He said she was evidently fatigued or she would not have spoken so abruptly."

"Well, there you are. She's fatigued and needs rest," said Henry Francis.

Robin continued to argue. "I don't see why she's so tired. She hasn't been doing very much lately."

"Spending less time with her younger brother, Robin, doesn't mean Philippa's been less occupied than usual. She has more important—and enjoyable—things to do than taking you for a stroll in the Park. I don't want to hear any more complaints."

Robin fell silent, impressed by Henry Francis's severity. Clarissa was braver, though, and muttered a soft protest in her younger brother's ear.

"I'd still like to know what more important things Philippa's been doing. She spends all her time alone in her bedroom. I shouldn't think *that's* too enjoyable!"

Henry Francis glanced sharply at his sister and brother. They smiled at him as innocently as they could. Henry Francis sighed and called for their reckoning from the innkeeper. He disliked the city and, eager to see open fields again, had driven the children up to Hampstead for the afternoon. They were as heartily sick of London smells and crowds as he. Isabella had sketched a view of the Heath quite prettily; Clarissa had wound early primroses into a three-foot-long chain; Robin had lost a kite to a tall, unscalable tree. It was not until Isabella reminded Henry Francis that he was expected to escort his sister to Almack's that evening that he had taken the children to an inn for a hurried dinner. They ate the cold meats and the game pie quickly, and Henry Francis wasted no time during the drive home. Nevertheless, it was fully half-past eight when they returned to Half Moon Street.

"Philippa will be furious," Isabella prophesied. "You were supposed to go to Blawith House with her at eight."

Henry Francis irritably told her to hold her tongue. He ran in and found Philippa waiting in her bedroom.

"I'm sorry, my dear. We lost track of time during our pleasant outing."

"It's no matter."

Henry Francis retired to his own room and hastily donned the kneebreeches and stockings required for an evening at Almack's Assembly Rooms. He returned to his sister's bedroom some fifteen minutes later. She was still sitting there, her concession to impatience the knots she was idly tying in the fringe of her shawl of Norwich silk. She wore the dashing costume Petherton had laid out for her: a pure white dress that ended some inches below the knee, allowing the several bands of dark red velvet on her muslin petticoat to show through. Her shawl too was white, but she wore garnets that had belonged to her mother in her ears and round her neck. Her hair was curled *à la Ninon,* loosely bound with a red velvet ribbon.

"Very Parisian, my dear," Henry Francis told her as he helped her up into the carriage. Philippa gave him a short smile.

"Thank you, Henry. I love wearing Mother's garnets. I hope Carlington won't be too impatient with us."

"I shouldn't think he'll mind our tardiness, my dear. His mother—I must tell you candidly I walk in terror of the Marchioness—or Lord Charles, perhaps, but the Earl, after all, is in love with you. He will excuse your little peccadilloes—now and after your marriage."

Henry Francis was hardly speaking seriously, but Philippa flushed and her reply was cold.

"I trust my behaviour shall not be such as to require excuses. Now or after our marriage."

Henry Francis was silent as they drove up to Grosvenor Street. Philippa, he thought unhappily, was not herself tonight.

Carlington and his family were waiting in the drawing-room for the Winslows to arrive.

"What a delightful evening this should be." Lady Blawith sighed. "Your first appearance in public with your *fiancée*, George. Everyone will watch as you dance—you must mind your steps. Miss Winslow is an exquisite dancer."

Lord Charles laughed. "Don't quiz George about his dancing, *maman*. He can't help inheriting our sire's lamented maladroitness."

"And I don't think it will matter too much in the House," Lady Blawith consoled her elder son. "Politics differs from the army in that respect. From all accounts, Wellington's men spent by far the greater portion of their time dancing. So fortunate, Charles, you inherited my fondness for it."

Lord Charles swept a bow to his mother. "I assure you the splendour of my military career, Mother, is due primarily to that legacy."

Lady Blawith chuckled. "I only wish I could waltz. Positively indecorous, of course, but what an exciting dance!"

"Stand up with me for it, Mother. I dare you to!"

Lady Blawith laughed at her younger son's proposal, but the Earl was considerably shocked.

"Charles! Consider the impropriety of the Marchioness of Blawith *waltzing*. The dance can only be engaged in by the very young, and even then I must confess to grave doubts . . ."

"But if Mother would enjoy it, George!"

"I shouldn't at all, Charles, and you know it. I'm far too old. And I don't know the steps," the Marchioness said on a practical note. "Think what a cake I'd make of you! After all, Charles, this is *your* first appearance at Almack's. You must make a good impression, selecting a skillful partner!"

"I'God, Mother, I've been to Almack's before. During the Long Vac, I think."

"But that was dog-years ago! If you were still at Oxford, you can hardly have been twenty!"

"I was twenty-one, Mother. The year I bought a commission."

Lord Charles wondered if he should break to his mother his plan to leave the country. He had told Carlington, who had been decidedly unenthusiastic about it. He foresaw some unpleasant scenes and reflected that it was probably best to tell his mother at the last possible moment.

"Isn't that carriage drawing up?" he asked. "Let's hope it's the Winslows at last."

It was, and the entire party went on to Almack's. Lady Blawith kept up a cheerful conversation, regaling them with the latest crim. con. stories, but, she noticed, everyone except the Earl seemed curiously preoccupied in his or her own thoughts. The Earl listened disapprovingly to his mother's store of gossip, and then remonstrated with her on the evils of spreading rumors until they reached the Assembly Rooms.

Almack's was crowded every Wednesday night, but this night was an extraordinary crush. It had been the scene of a quite appalling scandal the week before, when Lady Jersey, who thought she could manage everything to her liking in this most exclusive of London clubs, had tried to restore Lord Byron, whose misdeeds were notorious, to public favour. She had failed miserably, and this week all the *ton* had come to Almack's to see how she had taken her failure.

"Sally Jersey looks perfectly composed," Lady Blawith commented as her party entered. "Do you see her? By the window, talking to dear Helena."

"Oh, is Helena here?" Henry Francis exclaimed.

Philippa turned to Lord Carlington.

"Henry hates to dance with ladies he does not know. You just watch—he'll stick with Cousin Helena for as long as she can bear it, and then he'll retire to the refreshment room."

"I didn't want to come," Henry Francis defended himself. "My sister's a managing female, Carlington. Dragged a promise out of me to accompany her. But I'll go see Cousin Helena. Your servant, ma'am."

He bowed to the Marchioness and crossed the room to where his cousin, looking elegant in a robe of straw-coloured satin, stood. Lady Helena readily accepted his invitation to dance; within moments Henry Francis was confiding to her his worries about Philippa.

"She seems tired, somehow languid, all the time," he explained.

"Languid! How very unlike Philippa!"

"Yes, it's extraordinary. Ever since her betrothal."

Lady Helena frowned.

"Perhaps it's only to be expected," she said judiciously, "that a young girl may feel dismayed at the prospect of settling down to domesticity. Philippa enjoys racketing about so much."

"That's true. I hadn't thought of that. And I suppose it's natural for a woman to be nervous before her wedding. Although I can't say Julia—Miss Phelps, you understand —has shown any apprehensions!"

"Ah, but Miss Phelps has known you all her life, Cousin Henry."

"And I'm such a mild-mannered, unalarming sort!"

"Quite."

Lady Helena smiled at her cousin, but she gazed over her shoulder at Philippa and the Earl. They were dancing now. Lady Helena saw with amusement that Lord Carlington was counting to himself as he came to a particularly difficult series of steps in the gay country dance the orchestra was playing. She could no longer conceal from herself her doubts about this match. They looked beautiful. Philippa was dancing, as always, with effortless grace, and Lord Carlington's face was lit up with a rare smile, proud of his partner and triumphant in his betrothal. Nevertheless, Lady Helena thought, she could not believe they were well suited to one another. Lady Helena hoped—and was surprised at herself for the fervour with which she hoped—that Philippa would realize her error before it was too late, before she and the Earl were irrevocably committed to life together. Then she shook herself. They were irrevocably committed, or as close to it as made no matter. And it was no concern of hers.

Don Fernando de Santiago y Anandas stood against the wall. His arms folded, he glowered at anyone unwary enough to address him. He watched Philippa dancing with Lord Carlington, angrily following her every motion with his eyes.

"How do you do, Don Fernando?" a pleasant voice beside him asked.

Don Fernando turned, scowling, to face Lord Charles.

"They do make a pretty pair, my brother and Miss Winslow, don't they?" Lord Charles imperturbably continued.

Don Fernando continued to scowl. This young Englishman evidently expected him to utter some polite comment on Miss Winslow's betrothal. Don Fernando's soul revolted against such hypocrisy. He would show this young man with the infuriating smile that he, alone in this cold land, was not afraid to say what was in his heart. Don Fernando gazed at Philippa and murmured in soft tones some lines from Lord Byron's poem to his estranged wife, which had been published in a public newspaper the day before, shocking all London.

"Every feeling hath been shaken/Pride, which not a world could bow/Bows to thee—by thee forsaken/Even my soul forsakes me now."

Lord Charles was considerably impressed by this feat of memory. Not to be outdone, he affected a cynical smile. "Maidens, like moths, are caught by glare/And Mammon wins his way where Seraphs might despair," he intoned.

Don Fernando looked at him in astonishment.

"I beg your pardon?"

"*Childe Harold,* the first canto, ninth stanza," Lord Charles obligingly explained.

"I did not know English soldiers read poetry."

"No, how should you?" Lord Charles smiled. "I'll admit few of them do."

"Charles is talking to that Spanish friend of yours," Lord Carlington informed his betrothed as they made their way down the long double line of an old-fashioned reel.

"Indeed?"

"I'm worried about Charles, my dear," he went on.

Philippa almost laughed. She was in no position to allay the Earl's fears about his brother, whatever they were. She could not imagine that he suspected Lord Charles of cheating at cards, but perhaps he had learned of some other disgraceful action. Philippa felt she knew as much as she wanted about Lord Charles's dissolute character.

"I should think your brother is too old, Lord Carlington, to worry about. If he can survive Waterloo, he can take care of himself," she said tartly.

"You don't understand, my dear Philippa. He is about to embark on the most ill-conceived undertaking!"

"I don't want to hear about it," Philippa said flatly.

Looking at Lord Carlington's injured expression, she relented.

"I'm not yet a member of your family, Carlington, and, as your brother has not chosen to confide his, er, ill-conceived undertaking to me, I feel uncomfortable being told of it."

"But I do need your help in dissuading him. Mother, who knows Charles so well, suggested your opinion might have some sway with him."

"I shouldn't think so."

"Well, we shall see," Lord Carlington said cheerfully as their dance ended. "Here we are right by Charles. Charles! Come dance with Miss Winslow. She won't credit your absurd plan until she hears it from your own lips."

Lord Charles's face paled. Philippa blushed. She seized on the first excuse that occurred to her.

"But I'm afraid I promised this dance to Don Fernando. Perhaps I shall dance with Lord Charles later."

Giving her hand to Don Fernando, who smiled knowingly, Philippa moved back toward the dance floor.

"Why did you do that?" Don Fernando asked her as soon as they were out of earshot. "Why don't you want to dance with your *fiancé's* brother?"

"Oh, he's a horrid man," Philippa said airily. "Always smiling—I can imagine nothing more irritating. But I'm sorry I entrapped you like this."

"Not at all, Miss Winslow. I haven't seen you since the announcement of your betrothal. Permit me to wish you joy on your so brilliant *coup*," he said with heavy sarcasm.

"Thank you."

"I should like to warn you, Miss Winslow, though. Your Earl is an Englishman. He has all the phlegm of the

English, all their nasty virtues, and he has all their faults. No Englishman can understand a woman. You will be bored with him. I beg of you, remember my offer. If at any time you realize this foolishness of this marriage, a word, a glance—and you can be mine."

Philippa was rather struck by this speech, but, as she privately felt that Don Fernando might prove quite as boring as Lord Carlington, she did not encourage the Spaniard.

"I cannot but be flattered by your offer, Don Fernando, but my mind is made up. I shall marry Lord Carlington, and I do not take kindly to strictures upon his character."

"I see. I will take you back to your admirable *fiancé*."

Don Fernando did just that, holding her hand and walking over to where Lord Carlington and Lord Charles were still engrossed in conversation.

"I return to you your betrothed," Don Fernando declaimed.

Philippa pulled her hand away from him in indignation.

"Ah, now you can dance with Charles," the Earl said happily.

"I'm really rather tired," Philippa said.

"After two dances! I insist you dance with Charles. And you must try to talk him out of his ridiculous project."

Philippa saw she would have to dance with Lord Charles, so she smiled and gave him her hand with no sign of discomfiture. Lord Charles did not smile; he silently led her to the floor.

"What is your ridiculous project, Lord Charles?" Philippa finally asked.

"Never mind. It's nothing to do with you," he said, lying.

Philippa looked up at him and ventured a quick smile. He remained impassive, and she looked down again.

Keeping her eyes carefully fixed just beyond his left shoulder, she spoke rapidly.

"I'm actually glad Carlington made us dance together. I've been thinking that I should talk to you."

"Why on earth, Miss Winslow?"

"You know perfectly well why!"

"I confess I haven't the slightest idea what you could wish to say to me."

"I must apologize to you, Lord Charles. I was far too emotional, too melodramatic, last Friday. You're my future husband's brother. You're Carlington's best friend. I'd forgotten that. He needs you—whatever you may be. And I liked you—before I knew what you were. I hope, for your brother's sake, that we can try to be friends."

Lord Charles suddenly lost patience with this rigamarole. He tightened his arms around her, and Philippa looked at him with wondering eyes.

"I don't want your friendship, Philippa," he said, softly, almost casually. "God damn it, you little fool, don't you know that I want your love?"

His voice was harsh as he finished his question. Philippa was speechless. They were at the edge of the crowd now. The dance was over. Lord Carlington and his mother were a few feet away. Lord Charles still held Philippa, his fingers bruising her arm. They stood silent. Philippa looked up into his eyes for a long moment. Then, with a little sob, she turned her head away. Lord Charles immediately released her.

"And that, Miss Winslow," he said with a bow, "is the real reason for my quixotic project."

"So Charles has told you his real reason," Lord Carlington merrily broke in, despite his mother's restraining hand on his arm. "Now you must tell me, Philippa."

He drew her to the dance floor. She waltzed mechanically, with none of her usual grace.

"But what is your brother's ridiculous plan?" Philippa asked quietly.

"He didn't tell you, after all? He hasn't told m'mother, either. She'll be furious. He's just returned, you know; she's hardly seen him. And one would think one member of the family in America is enough! All he says is that he's *ennuyé* with London. I told him that Antigua was certain to be a dashed sight more boring than London. But Charles never listens to me."

"He's going to Antigua?" Philippa asked numbly.

"Not if I can stop him! Or if Mother can, which is more to the point. She might be able to, although she wasn't able to stop him from joining the Army. Just out of the University, he was, and all afire to make his fortune killing Boney's men. Mother always hated having him away—and when he was lost in battle. That was the worst. . . ."

Lord Carlington rambled on. Philippa was not listening. Lord Charles was going to Antigua. Lord Charles loved her. It was nightmarish, this horrible tangle. She knew now, with terrifying clarity, that she loved Lord Charles. Of course she loved him. She'd probably loved him since their encounter in the innyard. She had thought she never wanted to see him again, but the thought of his departure was searingly, unbearably painful. He meant everything to her, and, she remembered with a start, he was a scoundrel. She had been prepared herself to be on amicable terms with him for his brother's sake, but he was unfit for any honourable man or woman to speak to. She loved him with all her heart, but she degraded herself in caring for him. Her love was hopeless. He was right to go to Antigua. He would be gone, and she could forget him and marry his brother.

She stopped short, missing a step. She had forgotten the man who held her in his arms. She would become the Countess of Carlington, the future Marchioness of Blawith. She would live with the Earl, share his bed, bear his children. She would doubtless help him write regular epistles to America to the brother on whom he lavished such misspent affection. Philippa rebelled against this future. Lord Charles had shattered the tidy, precise pattern she had made for her life. It was shattered beyond repair. She could never marry the Earl of Carlington.

Philippa wrenched herself, with a dry sob, from Lord Carlington's arms. She ran through the crowd to the door, oblivious to the cries and looks directed at her. Don Fernando stepped forward to meet her. He hoped Philippa would throw herself into his arms, but she brushed his hand away, unseeing. Lady Helena looked around for Henry Francis. She made her way quickly through the chattering crowd to the refreshment room to tell Philippa's brother what had happened. Lord Charles stood beside his mother. He watched Philippa with a curious frown. Lady Blawith muttered: "I'm sorry for the girl."

But Philippa had not looked back to see any of this. She ran into the street, not troubling to retrieve her pelisse. She called a hackney and directed it to Half Moon Street. She did not cry, but shivered convulsively as she stared out at the low-hanging fog that even the new gas-lamps did little to dispel. She had not even turned to see Lord Carlington, reddened and angry, standing alone in the middle of the great ballroom.

Chapter Thirteen

Henry Francis Winslow was impatient. No Corinthian, he drove his horses through the tiny village of Wimcombe at a pace that would have made Brownlow raise his hands in horror. Even so good a whip as Charles Staunton would not have dared cram the tired post horses round these corners, but Mr. Winslow was unaware of his audacity, hardly looking at what he was doing. It was nothing short of miraculous that he drove up to Wimcombe Manor without injury, just after ten in the morning.

Dismounting from his curricle, he loudly called for help. Holton was not long in coming out the door to greet his young master, but his anxious questions were forestalled.

"Yes, of course I'll be here for a few days. Have these taken round and rubbed down, will you? They are to go back to Watford. Is she here?"

Holton intimated that Miss Winslow had indeed arrived at Wimcombe very late the night before. Henry

Francis was halfway up the stairs when Holton called after him.

"Miss Phelps is here, Mr. Henry. She and Miss Philippa are in the east parlour."

"Thank you, Holton."

Henry Francis ran down the corridor and burst into the parlour.

"Philippa," he said furiously, "do you know what a trouble you've been?"

"I didn't expect you to come haring down here after me," Philippa calmly replied. "It's very kind of you, of course, but hardly necessary."

"*Your* journey was hardly necessary! Why the devil did you run away like this? Taking the common stage last night!"

"Don't browbeat your sister, Henry. She was in trouble, and tired of London. Of course she came back here."

Miss Phelps rose from her chair and crossed the room to where Philippa was standing. She slipped her arm through Philippa's and the two girls faced Henry Francis.

"Do close the door, Henry," Philippa said wearily. "I sent for Julia so I have her advice. I suppose I'll tell you my problem as well. But I don't think the servants need to know as well."

Henry Francis mutely obeyed.

"What is it, Philippa?" he asked gently.

"I was just telling Julia that she was right, weeks ago. I cannot marry Lord Carlington."

"Yes, that's what I thought the problem was. Philippa, my dear, Robin told you his story, didn't he? If you love the Earl, marry him! Don't let fine scruples about our father's unworthiness ruin your life. Carlington cares for you enough to survive even Father's unveiling as a cad."

"I don't think so," Philippa murmured. "He's so

conventional. He'll never forgive me for making a scene in Almack's last night."

"He will, Philippa! Just as he won't blame you for Father's crimes! Marry him!"

Philippa could not bear her brother's misreading of the situation.

"No, Henry! That's not it at all! Father didn't cheat."

"Oh, my God. You mean you don't know the story after all? I needn't have said anything."

"Of course I know the story. But Henry, you're wrong. Charles Staunton cheated."

Julia Phelps had been looking from one to the other with horrified eyes.

"Philippa," she reasonably said, "that doesn't make any sense. The Staunton family's one of the wealthiest in England. Charles Staunton can have no need to cheat at cards."

"And our dear father certainly does," Henry Francis interjected.

"I tell you, he told me himself! Lord Charles told me he cheated!"

Henry Francis whistled softly. He sat down heavily.

"Why did he tell you, Philippa?" he inquired.

"I—I don't really know."

Henry Francis, knitting his brows, spoke very slowly.

"It is shocking to hear this, Phil. More shocking, I must admit, than if I'd heard it of Father. But I don't see why it should stop your marriage. Even if you don't choose to tell the Earl—for he'll be heartbroken if he learns this —can't a wife keep secrets from her husband? At least when they're for his own good?"

"Oh, Henry, you don't understand! I don't want to marry Lord Carlington. I love his brother!"

Henry Francis rose from his chair. Julia put her arm around Philippa's shoulders.

"I love him! I love him and always will—and he's a blackguard!"

139

"Oh, my dear. How sad."

Henry Francis took his sister's arm and led her to a chair.

Julia said briskly, "You mustn't marry the Earl, Philippa. That much is clear."

"No, indeed," said Henry Francis.

Philippa passed her hand along her brow.

"I've been such a fool. All these weeks of plotting, *conspiring* to catch Carlington! Only to have my heart betray me! Straight out of one of Isabella's novels!"

"At least you've learned not to marry for money, my dear. And at least you've learned it in time," her brother told her.

"Oh, not at all. I must marry for money; I can never marry for love."

"Philippa, let me expose Lord Charles," Henry Francis said resolutely. "His brother should know he cheated."

"No, Henry! I couldn't bear that!"

"But he deserves disgrace, my dear. You must put him out of your mind."

"I shall put him out of my mind," Philippa said through her teeth. "But—oh, Henry, Carlington's been so good to me. I must shield Lord Charles if only to spare his brother that awful disillusionment. Especially when I am jilting him so flagrantly."

"Very well, my dear. I will respect your wishes. But I hope I shan't have to see Charles Staunton for a long time. I liked him! To think that he would stoop to cheating at cards!"

Philippa winced, and Julia turned on her betrothed.

"Don't, Henry. Don't talk to Philippa if you can't be more helpful than that!"

Henry Francis subsided. "You're right, Julia. I'm sorry, Phil. And I think you're well out of the match with Carlington. You are not really suited for him. Even if he had no brother, I can't believe the two of you would be happy together. And the children never liked him!"

Philippa looked up sharply.

"The children! Oh, how selfish I am! Self-indulgent! Letting my feelings outweigh common sense! I'm being ridiculous. Of course I must marry the Earl."

"Philippa!" Julia exclaimed. "It's not fair to him—his wife in love with his brother."

"Lord Charles leaves for Antigua next month," Philippa said steadily. "And I could make Carlington happy. He only fancies himself in love with me. You're right, Henry. I'm much too frivolous for him. He deserves a wife who can share his interests, someone of sober, serious habits, like Cousin Helena. But we could muddle along together. Perhaps I can grow less frivolous."

"Philippa, you should forget the Staunton family altogether. Stay here at Wimcombe for the rest of the season. You should rest."

"No, Henry. I'll marry the Earl in the teeth of it. I'd be a quixotic fool to throw away this marriage. We need it!"

"You'll be miserable! Forever!" was Julia's dire prophecy.

Philippa laughed, rather harshly.

"Oh, Julia! Always so sentimental! I promise you, my heart won't break. I have no doubt I shall get over this. Being a Countess, and a Marchioness, should compensate for a lot. Wealth, position, a worthy and affectionate husband. What more have I any right to demand? The children would be safe. That's what matters most.

Henry Francis took his sister's cold hand in his own.

"I don't want you to be martyred, Phil. We'll all live even if our land is put on the block and I hire myself out as a postboy! Don't feel compelled to marry the Earl!"

"I am compelled! Do you think I could live here, all of us subsisting in genteel poverty, with no chance for the children to escape, to do anything in the world? They could never do anything with their lives! We'd rot away here in Wimcombe, and I would always know I could have prevented it!"

There was no reply to this outburst; Henry Francis knew how true it was.

"And it's not all altruism, Henry! I don't want to live like that! I'd become a governess, I suppose! I'll be much better off with the Earl. And I don't want to live with guilt for the rest of my life. I don't want to know that because of some mad sentimentality I condemned my sisters and brothers to penury!"

Julia was the calmest of the three.

"There must be an alternative, Philippa," she said. "Surely you have other suitors. Can't you marry someone who isn't Lord Charles's brother? That Spaniard, perhaps?"

Philippa sprang out of her chair and hugged Julia.

"You're terribly clever, my dear! Of course! He's not as good-looking or well-born as the Earl, but how pleasant to be wafted off to Spain, never to see—anyone —again!"

"Philippa, he's old and foolish!" her brother expostulated. "You could never be happy."

"I'd be happier than I would be mailing Christmas gifts off to my husband's brother in Antigua, with a few carefully-penned words of affection!" she flashed.

"And the children!"

"Don Fernando's wealthy enough to settle them securely in life! And I shall take them with me to Spain. For some time, at least."

"You're mad! Think of what Father would say! It's a dreadful mistake!"

"Father will be only too delighted that I am marrying a wealthy man. I don't think he will pay attention to anything else, whomever I choose to marry!"

"Think about it for a while, Phil! Rest for a few days and you may realise what a fuss you are making over nothing!"

"Nothing! Nothing, Henry Francis! I think it's a splendid idea! I want nothing so much as to leave this country and everyone in it far behind me! I shall act on it at once."

"Philippa, you won't be losing anything by staying here for a few days," cried Henry Francis, alarmed that she might be planning to return to London immediately.

"I must do something, Henry! I can't just sit and watch life go by, with all my wasted opportunities! I must do something!"

"Haven't you had enough of matchmaking?" Henry Francis asked cruelly.

"You stay here at Wimcombe! You can stagnate and decay! I won't! And I won't let the children do so!"

Philippa, perilously close to tears, ran from the room.

Julia took Henry Francis's hand.

"Don't worry about her, my dear," she said. "She can hardly ensnare her Spaniard very quickly. After all, she's still betrothed to Lord Carlington. And is the Spaniard that impossible, Henry? I'm sorry I suggested it."

Henry Francis smiled down at his anxious *fiancée*. He dropped a kiss on her forehead.

"Thank Heaven you're not hot-headed and impulsive, Julia. Living with Phil can be very tiring. But she'll calm down soon, and think over it all quietly and sensibly. We needn't to worry."

Miss Phelps was reassured. She and Mr. Winslow spent the rest of the morning happily, without once thinking of Philippa.

Philippa had sought refuge in her bedroom. She pulled the door shut behind her and leaned against it, breathing hard. She sat down at the eighteenth-century escritoire that had been her grandmother's. She slowly took up a piece of cream-coloured writing-paper. She dipped her pen in the inkbottle and framed a letter, smoothly and without hesitation:

"*My dear Lord Carlington,*

"*I am deeply sensible of the honour you did me in asking me to become your wife. I hope you will believe that. Yet I am not worthy of your affection. I must ask you, my Lord, to terminate our engagement. I was wrong to let it go this far. I hope you can forgive me. With profound apologies,*

"*Philippa Winslow*"

She reread this, frowning, but found it acceptable. She sprinkled it with sand and, when the ink was dry, folded it over and inscribed it to The Earl of Carlington, Blawith House, Grosvenor Street, London.

Philippa pushed her chair back and looked out the window. The apple tree just outside her room had small buds on it. She smiled as she thought of how lovely it would look in a few weeks, covered with white blossoms. She walked across the room and flung up the windowsash. She leaned her elbows on the sill and took a deep breath of the fresh spring air. There were birds singing in the trees at the foot of the lawn. If she stood very still, she could hear the brook that ran through their proprety gurgling as it flowed. How comfortable it would be to slip into this enchanted, sweet-smelling world, forgetting all her duties and responsibilities. Then she squared her shoulders. Henry Francis would never have the energy to save their family, and her father simply didn't care if they all dwindled into genteel poverty. She was strong enough to save them all, and she would. She knew her duty, and she would fulfill it. A sense of righteousness was all she could hope for to sustain her through the lonely years ahead without Lord Charles. She blinked back her unruly tears and returned to her writing-table. Pulling out a new sheet of paper she calmly wrote:

"*My dear Don Fernando . . .*"

Chapter Fourteen

"There's no need to announce me," Helena Prescott, divesting herself of her pelisse and muff, firmly told the butler. "Lady Blawith asked me to come round."

Lady Helena hurried up the stairs to Lady Blawith's boudoir. That charming room was much more crowded than usual. When Helena entered, Lady Blawith waved away the maid brushing her long, silvery hair.

"Ah, Helena, how good of you to come round."

Helena stooped over and kissed the Marchioness's proffered cheek.

"But what is the matter, dear Lady Blawith? Your note sounded quite distraught."

The Earl, who was standing by his mother's satin-wood chaise longue, answered Lady Helena's question.

"You were at Almack's last night, Helena, when your cousin behaved in such an inexplicable—and, I may add, profoundly embarrassing—manner."

"Yes, of course, George, but I know no more than you what Philippa meant by it. I was quite shocked."

"I would not have thought it of Miss Winslow. She has always seemed such a prettily-mannered young lady. She must have had some very serious reason for enacting such a scene," Lady Blawith remarked thoughtfully.

"She hasn't looked quite the thing lately. Perhaps she is ill," Lady Helena suggested.

"Illness can hardly excuse such a Cheltenham tragedy," the Earl pontificated.

Lord Charles, who had been raptly gazing at the elaborate trellis-work design of improbably pink and yellow roses that covered the walls, spoke for the first time.

"My dear George, you mustn't allow your lacerated sensibilities to exaggerate the scene. Almack's has seen far more shocking behaviour—last week, for example—and I hardly think Miss Winslow's exploit will achieve the notoriety of Lord Byron or Caro Lamb's."

The Earl turned on his brother. "But I can't afford notoriety of any sort! A man in my position must not be a subject for scandal-mongers! I would never have expected such conduct from Philippa, the lady I had chosen to make my wife!

"Do you know, George," his brother drawled, "I would say that last night's scene was precisely in character for Miss Winslow. Hot-headed, undignified, rash—just what might have been expected."

Lady Blawith cast a curious glance at her younger son.

"Don't you even like Philippa?" Lady Helena faltered.

"I have just told you my estimation of her character," Lord Charles said roughly.

"I don't think we need to discuss Miss Winslow's character any further," the Marchioness blightingly said. "I asked you here, Helena, so that you might give us some advice. George received a letter by special messenger this afternoon. It's from Miss Winslow, from their place in the country—what's its name?"

"Wimcombe," Lady Helena replied. "Yes, I thought she'd gone down there when I was told this morning neither she nor Henry Francis were at home. He's doubtless gone after her. But what did the letter say?"

"She asks to be released from our betrothal," Lord Carlington explained. "Doesn't give a reason, either. Dashed peculiar."

Lady Helena heard this news with a rush of relief. She tried to keep her voice steady and reasonable as she answered.

"That does seem logical. Evidently she changed her mind about the marriage while dancing last night. Disgraceful conduct, but Philippa always was flighty."

"Yes, but why?" Lady Blawith implored. "It's ridiculous. George is a splendid catch for her—as he knows very well—and she up and leaves him in the middle of Almack's. She must have had some cause. What were you talking about, George?"

"Oh, family matters," the Earl unhelpfully replied.

"What family matters?" his mother persisted. "Something to do with her sisters and brothers?"

"No, no. It was nothing of importance."

"Don't you see, George, that that will provide some clue to your *fiancée's* abrupt *volte-face?* You must remember what you were discussing."

"If you must have it, Mamma, I was telling her of my brother's quixotic scheme of immigrating to the South Seas!"

"Not the South Seas, George, Antigua," Lord Charles mildly said. "And then perhaps Brazil. I'd like to see Father."

"Your brother's *what?*" Lady Blawith gasped. She

looked at Helena. A blinding light struck both of them at once.

"Of course," Helena murmured to herself. "How awkward. And yet how delightful!"

"I beg your pardon?" the Earl asked.

Helena was amazed at his lack of comprehension. Surely the solution was clear enough. She looked at the Marchioness, who, from the indulgent smile she was giving Lord Charles, had obviously found it. Lord Carlington, Helena reminded herself fairly, was not in possession of the vital clue—Philippa's and Lord Charles's first meeting at Watford.

"Nothing, nothing," Helena told the Earl.

Lord Charles looked sharply at his mother and then at Lady Helena. A small smile played about his lips. The Marchioness was the first to speak.

"The question is, my dear Helena: What shall be done now? Carlington was saying before you came in that he cannot believe this letter—"

"That a young lady should refuse the Earl of Carlington, such a pattern-card of all the virtues!" Lord Charles put in.

Lady Helena felt this confirmed her theory and glanced at the Marchioness. The Marchioness avoided her eye.

"I think," Lady Blawith said, "that Miss Winslow should be questioned about this decision. It is a weighty one, and she seems to have undertaken it very lightly."

Lady Helena stared at her, wondering what she was driving at. Then the Earl spoke.

"Surely, Mother, you don't expect me to drive all the way into Oxfordshire to remonstrate with Miss Winslow on her decision! It must be all of a three- or four-hour drive! Charles, you must know—she lives near Richard Briscoe. You were at Briscoe's just last month."

"It's a four-hour drive, I believe," Lord Charles blandly responded.

"In that case, Mother, it's quite impossible I should go this evening. You know I am expected at Lord Brougham's for dinner. A signal honour, and one I cannot refuse. Henry Brougham, you know, edits the *Edinburgh Review*. I shouldn't like to offend him."

"Tomorrow, then?" his mother persisted.

"I can't miss a day at Westminster with this furor over the Austrian question, Mother! Although I suppose if you really thought it necessary—"

Lady Helena stepped in here. "No, George, I don't think your mother could expect such sacrifice from you. You must be there when the tariff is debated. For the good of the nation! The Party needs you to argue its case!"

The Earl nodded. "That is true."

"Perhaps you could delegate someone," Lady Helena said delicately.

"Yes, indeed," Lady Blawith said. "You should send someone down to straighten matters with Miss Winslow, if only to tell her you quite concur in her decision."

Lord Charles, highly amused by these efforts on his behalf, was pleased to see that the Earl, who had not yet expressed his concurrence with Philippa's decision, nodded at his mother's statement.

"But who should I send?" the Earl asked. "It's a very delicate mission."

"I'd offer to go, of course," Lady Helena said, "but I do think the tidings would come better from a member of your family."

Lord Carlington turned to his brother. "Yes, indeed! Charles, would you go down to the country? Just to tell Miss Winslow I, er, release her freely from our betrothal, and all that."

Lord Charles sighed. "I'm engaged tomorrow night

for dinner, and I promised Tony Fortescue I'd go with him to Mendoza's fight in Richmond tomorrow," he lied.

"Tony won't mind," his mother urged. "And I do think you're the proper person to go."

"Well," Lord Charles sighed again, "if you *really* think I should, I suppose I must. For your sake, George."

"I shall be so grateful," the Earl told him warmly.

Lord Charles felt a pang of guilt, but firmly stifled it. He was busy turning over in his mind ways to convince Philippa he had not, after all, cheated at cards.

"Then that's all settled," his mother said happily. "It's a pity. I did like Miss Winslow, but I hardly think, George, she would have made a suitable wife for a man in your position! Running off in the middle of a dance!"

"No, indeed," the Earl said with a shudder. "Most inappropriate conduct in the wife of a Minister."

"Oh, George, you have hopes of the Cabinet!" Lady Helena exclaimed. "How wonderful!"

"I wouldn't say it's an immediate prospect, Helena," Lord Carlington seriously answered. "But I have done well by the Party, and I have confidence that the Party will do well by me."

"But you don't think the Government will fall, George?"

"The Prince Regent is on your side," the Earl grandly declared. "What that will mean for the future we can only surmise."

"The King is very old," Lord Charles cheerfully put in.

"I'm sure we're boring your mother, George. You simply must take me downstairs and tell me all about it!" Lady Helena told him.

"With pleasure, my dear," Lord Carlington replied, and she firmly propelled him out the door.

The Marchioness watched them with a quizzically raised eyebrow, but the moment the door was shut she whirled round to face her son.

"Charles, my dear! To think I didn't suspect! Although, to be sure, if you had told me you were sailing to Antigua I could have deduced your motive for that singularly cowardly plan."

"Cowardly?" Lord Charles queried.

"Cowardly," his mother relentlessly answered. "To think that a son of mine would give in so easily! Not that I would advocate stealing a bride from your brother, you know, if the two of them weren't so clearly ill-suited. You saw how relieved he was to get her letter! I don't think he could forgive anyone for making him look foolish in front of all London!"

"No, you're right. And I wonder about Lady Helena."

The Marchioness refused to be diverted. "And now that you have some evidence that Miss Winslow shares your feelings, well, nothing could be easier than arranging this affair between you. Carlington's pride will be wounded, but he'll recover. May even do him good. You must leave for Wimcombe at once."

"Hardly at once, Mother. After the rain yesterday, the roads'll be impassable after dark."

"It won't be dark for four or five hours!"

"There's another complication, Mother, that I shall have to try to clear up before I confront Philippa."

"But you will confront her? Charles, I am delighted with this! It would be better, of course, if she hadn't betrothed herself to George, but that's your own fault for staying abroad so long! You could have met her months ago!"

Lord Charles raised his hands. "Mother, I beg of you! Yes, it is a pity she promised to marry Carlington. Yes, I do love her with all my heart, but please, *maman*, don't speak of it until I see if she'll have me!"

"Oh, she must care for you."

"You are prejudiced. Not every lady sees me with your favourable eye!"

"She fled the room when George told her you were going half-way round the world to avoid her!"

"Mother, you don't understand." Lord Charles pushed some of the folds of his mother's sage-green dress off the chaise longue and sat down beside her. "Philippa thinks I cheated at cards last week."

"She's a fool, then," Lady Blawith tersely replied.

"Hardly, Mother. I told her so myself."

"Charles!"

Lord Charles told his mother the story. She was appalled.

"Of all the noddy-headed, chivalric things to do! Positively helping her to marry George! It makes me sick!"

"Mother, that's neither here nor there," Lord Charles patiently said. "Now I must hope I can convince Philippa I did lie."

"I shouldn't think that will be too difficult. But she's hard to handle—so impulsive. You would do well to get a confession from Sir Rupert."

"Ah, you too think Sir Rupert did it. Although the only other possibility is his son, who seems a bit of a prig. I suppose the deduction is not very great."

"No, not at all. Especially since I've known Rupert for years. I remember in Turin . . ."

"He's done it before, then? Good. It's nice to be sure that he did it before I try to surprise him into a confession."

"You mustn't rely on surprising him, dear. That's vulgar, as well as unreliable. Surely you can handle it with more *delicatesse*. As I said, I remember a story about Rupert in Turin—or was it BudaPesth?—in the spring of '82. . . ."

Lord Charles Staunton could be seen some minutes later strolling along Grosvenor Street, whistling cheerily.

He did not go to Half Moon Street, as he doubted very much the man he was seeking would be at home. He tried first Gentleman Jackson's pugilistic academy on Bond Street, and, when his inquiries there were fruitless, Daffy's Club. Daffy's was not yet open for the day, it being somewhat before five, but Lord Charles found the head porter, supervising the delivery of an order of oysters. He suggested Lord Charles try Tattersall's, where a prime stable was being put on auction that day. Lord Charles tipped him lavishly and strolled off toward Tattersall's, still joyful.

Tattersall's, that celebrated emporium for horseflesh and all appurtenances, was crowded with gentlemen of all description, most of whom had come not to bid but merely to see who did purchase these prizes from a bankrupt breeder's stable. An impressionable street-sweeper, as Lord Charles made for the establishment, informed him that no less a swell than the Regent himself had come to see the fun. Lord Charles threw the boy a coin, reflecting that this was an unexpected piece of luck. His quarry would certainly be in the circle surrounding the Prince, and it was only a matter of Lord Charles's getting through to that circle.

After much judicious elbowing and pushing, Lord Charles did at last find himself within hailing distance of his quarry.

"Sir Rupert," he bawled above the din. "Sir Rupert, may I speak to you for a moment?"

Sir Rupert thought at first that this stentorian cry came from one of his numerous creditors, and he jumped noticeably. When he located the man hailing him, however, he waved gaily and forced his way through the crowd.

"Hallo, Staunton. Glad to see you. How's y'r brother? Writin' more speeches to give old Metternich somethin' to think about, eh?"

"Quite," Lord Charles crisply said, and, taking Sir Rupert's elbow, forcibly steered him out of the crowd. When they were settled in a deserted showroom, filled with the latest high-perch phaetons and tilburies, Lord Charles asked Sir Rupert to sign a paper admitting that he had cheated at his own card-party.

"What the devil!" Sir Rupert sputtered. "Why should I do anything of the sort?"

"Well, you see, sir," Lord Charles, who was almost enjoying himself, explained, "I am in love with your daughter."

"Oh, that makes everything clear," said Sir Rupert with heavy sarcasm.

"I was fool enough, sir, to tell her that I cheated," Lord Charles imperturbably went on, "but I now wish to convince her of the mendacity of my earlier statement."

"The man's mad," Sir Rupert explained to no one in particular. "Even," he said carefully, "even if I were responsible, what the devil makes you think I would admit as much? In writing?"

"For one reason, sir, there is your daughter's happiness. For another, while I admit, sir, there is no proof as to this incident, there was a little affair in Turin, the year before you were married, I believe."

The next morning, Lord Charles drove out of London, a signed confession from Sir Rupert Winslow in his pocket. Sir Rupert had actually taken the whole thing in good humour. It would be very embarrassing for him to have the early incident exposed, as it involved no less a personage than the present King of Sardinia himself, but he found it amusing to be caught out. He shook hands with his blackmailer, saying that Lord Charles would be a distinct improvement over Lord Carlington as a son-in-law. He even, Lord Charles remembered with a smile as he deftly flicked his whip while rounding a corner, begged to have his best wishes sent to Lady Blawith. No doubt about it, Lord Charles thought to himself, I am perfectly suited to become a rogue of the first order. As he laughed merrily, he failed to notice the heavy travelling-coach with a foreign crest that whirled past him in a cloud of dust.

Chapter Fifteen

Lord Charles, unlike Mr. Winslow the day before, was not impatient. He drove at a leisurely pace through Wimcombe and alighted from his curricle with an easy leap when he reached the manorhouse. He once more ran over in his head what it was he would say to Philippa and boldly lifted the brass knocker on the front door. Holton opened it almost immediately.

"Is this Wimcombe Manor?" Lord Charles inquired.

"Yes, sir. Can I help you, sir?"

"I would like to see Miss Winslow, if you please."

Lord Charles handed the butler his card. To his surprise, Holton did not usher him into the house. The old man stood on the doorstep, dubiously regarding the card. Then he looked up at Lord Charles with an unfathomable expression.

Lord Charles knew a moment's panic. What if Philippa would not see him? What if she had left orders that he was not to be admitted? He was so horror-stricken by this possibility, which, oddly enough, had not occurred to him before, that he failed to grasp what Holton was telling him.

"You don't need to show me in," he said, fearing a rebuff. "I'll find my way myself."

Now, sizing up Lord Charles with a rapid eye, Holton was very sure that he knew why Miss Philippa had been so distressed and why she had descended on Wimcombe in such an unexpected and unorthodox manner. Jarvis, his colleague in London, had written to him that the entire household was jubilant over Miss Philippa's betrothal to the Earl of Carlington. Holton thought sourly to himself that Miss Philippa hadn't looked any too jubilant during the thirty-six hours she had spent at Wimcombe. And this dark young gentleman's feelings toward Miss Philippa were obvious enough. Smiling at Lord Charles, Holton said in a fatherly tone, "I'm afraid that wouldn't do, my Lord. Miss Philippa is not at home. She has, in fact, returned to the metropolis."

"Oh, my God!"

"If you wish, sir," Holton interposed helpfully, "I could take you in to Mr. Henry Francis."

"Yes," Lord Charles said quietly. "Yes, I suppose that would be best."

As he followed Holton up the staircase to Henry Francis's study, his mind was a whirl. His beloved, he thought, was really the most exasperating girl. He was so annoyed by this latest start of hers that, when, ushered in to a surprised Henry Francis's *sanctum sanctorum,* he burst out with the question on the tip of his tongue.

"What the devil is your sister doing in London?"

Henry Francis was not at all pleased by this interruption, particularly when, after he finished going over this set of accounts, he had planned to write a letter to the Earl of Carlington denouncing the very man who was now an unexpected and unwelcome visitor. He pushed the spectacles he had recently taken to wearing up on his sandy hair, pushed his old armchair away from his desk, and regarded the intruder with a baleful glance.

"By what right do you ask, Staunton?" he coldly inquired.

"What does that matter? What is she going to do?" Lord Charles hotly demanded.

"Today, sir, she is to wed Don Fernando de Santiago y Anandas in Saint Giles-in-the-Fields, by special licence, in"—Henry Francis pulled out his heavy gold watch—"precisely five hours."

"Damnation! You're not serious?"

"I assure you, sir, I am quite in earnest. I would also like to tell you that my sister has told me of your shocking admission and that I have every intention of informing Lord Carlington and the rest of the *haut-monde* of your conduct without delay."

This situation was too horrible to be true. It was incredible, Lord Charles thought. No one, no one, could be in as hellish a situation as this. Lord Charles sank into a chair, buried his face in his hands, and laughed convulsively, on the verge of hysteria. Henry Francis was affronted. A paltry fellow, this Staunton, he thought, although it was no doubt better to laugh when faced with ruin than to cry. Henry Francis, to whom being faced with ruin was not so remote a possibility, thought a dignified, stoic silence was the best course to take. Philippa, he thought idly, was not likely to agree. He did not know what she would do, but silence had never been her forte. She was much more likely to react emotionally, to throw something, perhaps to cry, or, Henry Francis thought with amusement, to laugh. Perhaps he could understand, after all, something of this wild attachment she seemed to have for Charles Staunton, and, from all indications, Charles Staunton had for her. They were similar in character—volatile people with a buoyant, laughing view of life.

Henry Francis, who had at one point considered

taking the cloth, reflected on this. They were wrong, he concluded; life was a serious matter, a solemn matter, complicated by profligate parents, sisters in ill-control of their emotions, and good-looking scapegraces like the man in front of him. He looked at Lord Charles's shaking shoulders with scant sympathy. The man had been born with all the advantages of rank and fortune and had squandered them all, bewitching Philippa in the process. He was a cad and a scoundrel, who could not in justice remain unindicted, and what fanned Henry Francis's resentment was that Philippa loved him all the same. He did her immeasurable harm by remaining in polite society. If he were outcast, perhaps Philippa, Dona Fernando, would be cured. Henry Francis steeled himself to leave the room without compunction for the man still laughing in the chair.

As he turned to go, Lord Charles, as he had feared, arose. Lord Charles did not, however, plead or bargain with Henry Francis, but mutely pulled a piece of paper from the pocket of his greatcoat and held it out. Henry Francis did not understand, but slowly took the paper and unfolded it. He started when he saw his father's flamboyant signature at the end, and quickly scanned the sheet, frowning. Then he looked up at Lord Charles, his face expressionless, and, articulating each word as if to impress it upon his memory, read it aloud, more to himself than to Lord Charles.

"I, Rupert Winslow, do hereby affirm that, on the night of April the sixteenth, in the year eighteen hundred and sixteen, at a card-party in my home, I did willfully and maliciously cheat at a game of cards, for base profit." Here Henry Francis remembered his audience and looked up, smiling wryly. "Don't tell me you dictated this. I detect Father's hand."

Lord Charles merely nodded, and Henry Francis painfully went on. *"I alone did so, and all other persons attendant at that party are completely and totally innocent of any such charge."*

Henry Francis thoughtfully refolded the paper, and, still holding it in his hand, meekly asked: "What does this mean?"

"I shan't denounce him," Lord Charles said quickly. "You needn't fear that. I couldn't do that to Miss Winslow."

Henry Francis's reaction, his austere principles forgotten, was one of unadulterated relief. Sir Rupert might deserve public scorn at least as richly as Lord Charles did, but Henry Francis did not want his family ruined. Don Fernando's money, it was true, would help a great deal in the event of such a scandal, but, without noble connections or resources in England, none of the children could ever hope to move in the society their father had betrayed.

Then he realized the significance of Lord Charles's last statement.

"Then you love her?" he asked. "You do, don't you?"

Lord Charles had had quite enough of feinting and lying and replied frankly, "Yes, yes, I do. More than all the world."

"Well then, you have things to do!" Henry Francis cheerfully exclaimed, his instinctive liking for Charles Staunton coming to the surface once more.

Lord Charles was bewildered by this change of fronts. He had reseated himself in the capacious wing-chair, and from its leather depths he replied dolefully: "I can't imagine what. Your sister will go to Spain with that *poseur*. I shall go to Antigua."

"Then you're a fool. She loves you, of course. Why do you think she ran out of Almack's? She's breaking her heart over you."

Lord Charles leaped out of his chair. He grabbed Henry Francis by the shoulders. "Did she tell you that? How do you know? What did she say? Why is she marrying that damned Spaniard?"

Henry Francis was undisturbed by this and placidly adjured Lord Charles to stop making so much noise. "Of course she told me. I'm not much for drawing deductions. She told me she loved you, but that you were a cad, and now she's gone off to marry that prosy Spaniard. For his money, of course. Feels she must, for the children's sake."

"My God, what a fool I've been!"

"Yes, quite," Henry Francis agreed, "although m'sister hasn't been much better. Apparently Don Fernando offered for her some weeks ago. She wrote to him, accepting his proposal, at the same time she wrote to your brother. He came down last night and took her up to London a few hours ago. Fools the pair of you, which is all the more reason matters shouldn't be left in your hands. We're going to London now."

There was a light of hope in Lord Charles's eye, but it was speedily quenched. "It's no good, Winslow. Oh, maybe we'd make it to London in time, but we can't stop the wedding. She'll marry that ass, and she'll regret it."

It was an ironic change, an observer would have noted, in the two men's usual characters. Henry Francis, was for once aflame inspired to action by his affection for his sister, sure she could be saved from this disastrous marriage, and also sure, for the first time since the afternoon in Richmond, that all would end happily ever after for her. Lord Charles, for the first time in his life, felt himself up against something he couldn't handle. He had no more hope left; the shocks of these recurring changes had left him passive. He had thought only an hour before that, against all odds, Philippa might yet be his; he now was resigned to losing her. He had never really had much chance of winning her. She had broken off one misguided betrothal, which was more than he had dared to hope, and he could not dare to think that this one too might yet be reconsidered.

Henry Francis would not permit Lord Charles the luxury of this apathy. Lord Charles's face had gone very white, he saw with compassion, and he rang for Holton.

"I shall get you some brandy, and then we shall drive up to London," Henry Francis calmly stated. Looking at Lord Charles's long, crumpled figure, he said gruffly: "Look here, you may fancy making a may-game of my sister's marriage vows in a few months, but I don't. We're going to do our damnedest to see she doesn't marry this fellow, because I'll never forgive myself if she does. I thought it was a mistake, but was content to sit here sulking when I thought you, er, ineligible. I'll be damned if I'll let it happen now. I know what would happen between you, or what might happen when you met again, and I won't have it. If not for her sake, for the children's. They'd be ruined, just as effectively as by my father's crime, and they think a lot more of Phil than they do of Father."

Lord Charles had looked up sharply at the beginning of this speech, but he did not try to refute it.

"Very well," he murmured. "I'm with you." He disentangled himself from the chair in which he had slumped and stood, a little shakily, one hand on the back of the chair.

"Ah, Holton," Henry Francis said as the butler appeared. "Bring us some brandy, will you? And have my horses put to Lord Charles's curricle—I presume you came by curricle, Staunton?—as we are to return to London. And, Holton, hurry!"

"Yes, sir." Holton made to leave, but, his hand on the doorknob, turned to Lord Charles. "May I say, sir, I wish you the best of luck, and all happiness."

Charles laughed slightly bitterly and, when the door had closed behind Holton, muttered: "How the devil did he know?"

"I won't bore you, my dear chap, by saying that your feelings are somewhat evident," Henry Francis airily replied. "Your horses, who are no doubt happily champing on country hay, can stay here for a while. They must be worn out. Mine aren't as good, but at least they're fresh. You must be tired too, but I'm afraid you'll have to drive. *I'm* no top-sawyer."

Lord Charles smiled and said, "Perhaps we can set a record."

"Perhaps indeed," Henry Francis replied.

"What are you doing here, anyway?" Lord Charles curiously asked. "Did your stomach turn that much at the thought of watching her wed that Iberian?"

"Yes," Henry Francis explained with a heartfelt sigh. "She wasn't too pleased, but admitted it wouldn't be the most edifying or cheerful spectacle."

This raised Lord Charles's spirits immensely; he grinned stupidly and itched to set off.

Holton re-entered with the brandy and Lord Charles gratefully emptied the glass at one gulp.

"Are the horses ready, Holton?"

"Just about, sir."

Lord Charles smiled at him and ran down the steps two at a time. Henry Francis followed at a more sedate pace, and jumped up beside Lord Charles in the perch-seat. Lord Charles cracked the reins and, with fearful precision, swerved round and through the iron gates without a moment's hesitation. A stableboy whistled at the feat, but Lord Charles was oblivious to him. Lord Charles was concentrating fiercely, unlike his ride down. The world had narrowed to the two handsome and obedient bays before him and the endless ribbon of road that stretched out between him and his beloved. Henry Francis smiled when he glanced at Lord Charles's frowning brows. They would get there in time; Charles Staunton had set his mind to it.

Chapter Sixteen

At the same moment, miles away, Jarvis ushered the Marchioness of Blawith into Sir Rupert Winslow's study. Sir Rupert was at his ease in an old armchair, studying a dog-eared *Guide to the Turf*. He rose with some surprise when Lady Blawith was announced.

"My dear Honoria, I can't have seen you in the last decade!"

He kissed her warmly and motioned her to a comfortable chair. "Doubtless not," she replied. "I was in South America with my husband for some time, and since then I have principally resided at Pembley."

"Understandable," Sir Rupert frankly responded. "Shouldn't want to live with that son of yours myself." As Lady Blawith looked somewhat offended, he tried to amend matters. "Not that I'm not fond of young Charles. Regular out-and-outer he is, not at all like Carlington. Nearly floored me when he taxed me with that old story yesterday. Clever thing to do!"

"Gracious, Rupert!" Lady Blawith said with some amusement. "Who do you think thought of it? I'll never forget that evening in Turin!"

"I'd like to," Sir Rupert smiled engagingly. "But I can't—as you very well know."

"I am sorry about that—but it was blackmail in a good cause. I'm delighted with their betrothal."

"Young Charles can support m'daughter, I assume."

"Oh, yes, Rupert. Pembley will go to Carlington along with the title, of course, but Charles gets half his grandfather's money. And he's got a lot from my brother, too. There's no problem there. I am overjoyed that he's settling down now."

"I don't know how *settled* living with my minx will be!"

"Even the most adventurous domestic bliss has to be better than following the Duke over half of Europe! Philippa may lead him a sad dance, but he's finished with wars."

"And from what I've seen of your son, Honoria, I think he can control Philippa."

Lady Blawith smiled. "Charles can. George couldn't have. I am glad that's off."

"To tell you the truth, it's a pity my girl won't be a Marchioness some day! Lady Charles Staunton doesn't have the ring of the Countess of Carlington!"

"Or Marchioness of Blawith! I know. But I don't think Philippa will mind. I shall write to Adelaide tonight. She *will* be pleased."

"My daughter marrying your son. Yes, that will please Adelaide."

"It's remembering Adelaide that makes me so glad Philippa won't marry George. Not that George would ever *immure* Philippa the way the Graf did Adelaide, but marrying for money must always be a mistake!"

At this inauspicious moment, Philippa burst into the room. She had run up the stairs.

"Father, thank heaven you're home! I'm—well, I'm going to marry Don Fernando, not the Lord Carlington!"

Philippa had not seen Lady Blawith, who now rose from her chair.

"You are marrying Don Fernando de Santiago y Anandas?" she inquired awfully.

Philippa went very white.

"Oh, I do beg your pardon, ma'am. I wasn't aware my father had a visitor. I'm just leaving anyway."

She opened the door she had imperiously slammed shut a moment before.

"No! Damme, Philippa, you're not walking out of here cool as a cucumber after that announcement! I demand to know what's going on in this household!"

"I have just explained to you, Father," Philippa replied coolly. "I am marrying Don Fernando at St. Giles-in-the-Fields at five o'clock today. Lady Blawith, this must be rather a shock to you if your son has not taken you into his confidence. I wrote to him yesterday morning, terminating our betrothal."

"I'd gathered as much from Charles Staunton," her father said. "But why the devil marry this Spaniard? Or break off with Carlington, for that matter?"

Philippa winced at the mention of Lord Charles. With as much dignity as she could muster, she said, "Pray do not ask my reasons, Father. I certainly shall not tell them to you. Lady Blawith, I am sorry for this encounter, which must be as painful for you as it is for me. Good day."

Before either of them could stop her and ask the question burning on their lips—had Lord Charles spoken to her?—she had turned to leave.

Her father called after her, "Where the devil do you think you're going, my girl?"

"To the school-room, of course, to tell the children. I imagine they would like to attend the ceremony. You may also, if you like, Father. Henry Francis stayed at

Wimcombe, so I need someone to give me away. Five o'clock." And she closed the door firmly behind her.

Lady Helena Prescott had spent the morning at her milliner's, Eulalie, in Bond Street. It was a glorious day—fresh and warm and clear. Spring is finally here, she had told herself. In celebration, she had bought the little chip bonnet decorated with cherry-coloured ribbons she had admired, but condemned as hopelessly juvenile, the week before. Now she walked happily down Bond Street, decorously followed by a footman, who carried her parcel. She wore a gown of her favourite lavender, with only the lightest of pelisses over it. She greeted acquaintances cheerfully and idly wondered what Philippa had told Lord Charles at Wimcombe and why today, of all days, seemed so particularly glorious. She even waved a hand gaily at Don Fernando de Santiago y Anandas, whom she privately considered to be rather low-bred, when she saw him, florid and glossy in his best clothes (with an astonishing number of fobs on his gorgeously embroidered waistcoat) leaving his jeweler's, Rundell and Bridges.

"Ah, my lady, how fortunate it is that I should meet you!" Don Fernando kissed Lady Helena's hand. She was surprised and withdrew it with some disdain.

"I beg your pardon, Don Fernando? *Why* is it so fortunate?"

Her tone would have quelled a more sensitive man than Don Fernando, but he answered with unimpaired amiability.

"Now I have the great honour, Milady Helena, of inviting you to my wedding."

"I beg your pardon?" Lady Helena repeated. "Why, sir, should I have any interest in attending your wedding?"

Don Fernando smiled broadly. "I, ma'am, have been blessed by your cousin! She has granted finally to me the dearest wish of my heart."

"Heavens! You don't mean Philippa . . ." Lady Helena's voice trailed off pathetically.

"We are to be married at five o'clock. I have obtained a special license. Tonight we shall spend in my chambers at The Albany. Next week, we shall set sail for Spain."

"But, my dear sir, this is so sudden!"

"*I* have not been sudden. I have loved Miss Winslow for aeons, millennia!"

"It's certainly sudden on *her* part! The day before yesterday she was betrothed to the Earl of Carlington! This is scandalous!"

"I am sorry you take that attitude, Lady Helena. I had hoped you would attend our modest ceremony. I know it would make dearest Philippa happy."

"I should not dream of attending! Condoning such a shocking alliance! I am disgusted! Good day, sir. I shall call on Philippa at once and tell her what I think of this latest escapade."

Don Fernando was quite unsnubbable.

"May I offer you my escort to Half Moon Street, Lady Helena? I am calling on Miss Winslow myself."

"Surely that's not necessary four hours before your marriage, Don Fernando?"

"Ah, but I have not yet presented her with an engagement ring. A plain gold wedding band is tonnish, but my bride must have jewels! So I have purchased for her the most splendid ring Rundell and Bridges had to offer!"

"Oh, indeed."

Don Fernando proudly took a velvet jewel case from his pocket and before Lady Helena could protest flipped it open to reveal a glittering and heavy diamond ring.

"Rather gaudy, isn't it, sir? I don't think I shall call on my cousin after all. I do wish you two joy of one another."

Her footman whistled softly; he had never heard

Lady Helena so acerbic. Don Fernando was hurt. He gave Lady Helena the sketchiest of bows and stalked away. Lady Helena stood in the middle of Bond Street, thinking deeply.

"I don't like to disturb him," she said to herself. "He's well out of the affair. But he must know. It is my duty to tell him."

Lady Helena, obeying her conscience as she always did, turned west and walked quickly toward Grosvenor Street.

Philippa was finding her explanation to the children hard going.

"You see, I've decided to marry Don Fernando, not Lord Carlington," Philippa explained after her first announcement—that she was to be married that day rather than a month later—had been greeted with incredulous silence.

"Why? That's very silly!" Robin severely said.

"Not really, sweetheart. I must marry, and I've simply changed my mind as to whom."

"But why be married today? It will be a dreadful scandal," Isabella shrewdly remarked.

"In all candour, I don't really care."

"Then neither do I," said Clarissa. "Can I carry flowers for you?"

Philippa kissed her little sister.

"If you don't," she solemnly assured her, "I shall burst into tears in the middle of the ceremony. My wedding without Clarissa bearing flowers! Unthinkable."

"I hope you want me, too," Isabella said stiffly.

Philippa hugged her. "You know perfectly well I shouldn't dream of marrying without all three of you present. And I'm absolutely furious with Henry Francis for staying at Wimcombe!"

Sir Rupert entered without knocking.

"Father," exclaimed Clarissa. "Have you heard Philippa's news?"

"You'll be there, won't you?" Robin asked.

Sir Rupert hardly looked at them.

"Out, children!"

"Father, this is our room!"

"Robin, out! I must speak to Philippa."

"You can do that with us in the room," Clarissa said pertly.

"Children," Philippa said, "please go."

They reluctantly obeyed. Sir Rupert closed the door behind them. "Sit down, Philippa," he said. "I have something of great importance to tell you."

Chapter Seventeen

Philippa lifted her chin. "Don't tell me not to marry Don Fernando, Father. My mind is made up. I cannot imagine that you will be so blind to your own self-interest as to withhold your consent."

"Philippa! Don't you speak to me like that! Not that you're not right. You can marry that Iberian if you want to—I'm told he's quite a catch. But I wanted to talk to you about Charles Staunton."

"What can you have to tell me about Lord Charles? He doesn't enter into this at all!"

"A pity, m'dear. Can't help but think he'd be a more amusin' son-in-law."

"There was never the least question of that, Father," she replied with *hauteur*.

"He hasn't spoken to you?"

Philippa's answer was cold. "Father, Lord Charles and I have nothing to say to one another."

"He didn't cheat at cards, Philippa," Sir Rupert said quickly.

Philippa stared. "How do you know about that?"

Sir Rupert prepared himself for a momentous announcement. He put his hand on Philippa's shoulder and guided her to a seat. He took a dramatic stance in front of the fireplace. The sunlight, streaming through the barred windows, fell directly on him, and Philippa remembered how old he was. He brushed some imaginary soot off his impeccably tied cravat and cleared his throat. Philippa sat docilely in a state of total confusion.

"You have unjustly suspected Lord Charles."

"How do you know, Father? I don't understand."

"That is because, my dear, you are unaware of the key feature of this sorry affair. That is—and I am sorry to break it to you, but it is better that you should hear it from a loving father than from a stranger—that it was I who marked the winning card."

"Father!"

"I blush to admit it," Sir Rupert said, although any observer less preoccupied than Philippa would have seen that this was far from the case, "but it is true. I am the guilty one. I am he who must take the blame."

Philippa was not affected by the news of her father's crime the way a well brought-up young lady should be. She sprang from her chair and stood erect.

"Lord Charles didn't cheat, Father? He didn't?" she asked tremulously.

"Well, of course he didn't," her father testily said. "Haven't I just finished telling you that?"

"But why? Why did he tell me he did? And how do you know about it?"

"I infer, m'dear, that he wanted to shield you from the consequences of my impulsive action."

"How do you know?"

"He came by yesterday, badgering me for a confession."

174

"But why, why now?"

"I assume he had learned that you had asked to be leased from your promise to his brother."

"But this is wonderful!" Philippa threw her arms ound her father. "Father, dear, that means he loves me! nd I love him! I must go to Blawith House at once."

"He won't be there, Philippa."

"I beg your pardon?"

"He planned to drive down to Wimcombe this orning to meet you. With a signed confession from me his pocket."

Philippa laughed merrily. "How impulsive! I do hope enry Francis will tell him where I am! Do you know, m tempted to return to Wimcombe at once! But I sup-
ɔse he'll be on his way back to London."

"Yes, and he's probably in a damned bad temper!"

"At missing me? I think it's funny!"

"Take a damper, my girl!" Sir Rupert roughly ad-
sed. "Have you forgotten that you are planning to
pouse that windbag of an Iberian this very day? Your
ind was made up," he added, with heavy irony.

"Dear God in Heaven!" Philippa stopped short in
er exultant dance around the room. "How can I ever
xplain this away?"

"You can't. Staunton would do well to give up on
ɔu. Marrying a man at the drop of a hat! It'll be the talk
f the town, after you've jilted the Earl! Don't know how
:aunton could marry you in the teeth of that."

"It's his fault," Philippa said. "If he hadn't told such
stupid lie, this wouldn't have happened."

"You had already promised to marry the Earl."

Philippa did not appreciate the justness of this state-
ent.

"Father, it's all your fault, really! Don't criticize my
ɔnduct! I'd like to know what we're to do with you!"

"I beg your pardon?" Sir Rupert asked warily. "Do
ɔu have anything in mind?"

"I think—Father, I think it would be best if you lef
the country. Don't you?"

"Philippa, m'dear, I am very fond of you. I know
what I've done, and I regret it, for your sake. Where
would you have me go?"

"You could visit Cousin Adelaide in Bonn. The
Continent's safe now."

"But, my dear, of all the dull towns in Germany
Bonn . . ."

"I know, I know, but don't you think that's what yo
need? You could write your memoirs there, and you lik
Cousin Adelaide, even if she disapproves of modern so
ciety. Think what fun it would be to write your memoir:
You've been planning them for years."

Sir Rupert, remembering the chequered career i
which he had known everyone of importance in Europea
society in the last thirty years, thought his daughter migl
well be right. Cousin Adelaide, widow of the Graf vo
Lansdorfer, had been a great beauty and a crony of his i
his youth. She had secluded herself in her townhouse i
Bonn after her German husband's death, but she woul
welcome him warmly, he knew. He could live there chear
ly, and he was, after all, growing old. Fashionable societ
was more tiresome each year, and the people and manne:
of today were hardly to be compared to those of the gli
tering world of his youth. Yes, he would like to talk ove
old times with Adelaide, who, despite her life of the u
most propriety, was never shocked at anything he said
He would go to Bonn, and so he told his daughter.

"I'm so glad, Father. I'll write to Cousin Adelaic
tonight."

"And you can come visit us after your wedding tou
Philippa. If you ever get married."

"If, indeed," Philippa sighed. "This is not going to b
a pleasant afternoon. I can't marry Don Fernando. I on
hope he doesn't take it too badly. And that Lord Charl
comes back soon."

"It will work out, Philippa," her father consoled her. "Charles Staunton, I would guess, gets what he wants."

"Oh, Papa," Philippa said lovingly. "You're a scoundrel, you know, but I do love you. And you will behave yourself with Cousin Adelaide?"

"You've met Adelaide, m'dear, although it was quite a while ago. You should know that I shan't have any choice."

"All the better!" Philippa retorted. She was in a terrible scrape, but now she was happy, far too happy to chide her disgraceful and not very repentant father. "I shall send a note round to Don Fernando, asking him to come here immediately."

"He'll think it is bad luck," Sir Rupert pointed out. "Catholics are always superstitious."

"It's improper, I know, but I don't want to send him a letter. That would be the easy way out—I'll have to extricate myself from this in person."

"Don't worry, m'dear," Sir Rupert jovially said, slapping her on the shoulder. "He can't hold you to your promise against your will, you know. All that will happen is that you'll look a fool, which has happened before."

"Often enough," Philippa said ruefully. "But I hope Lord Charles returns."

"He will, he will," Sir Rupert assured her with all his characteristic confidence. "He'll be back in London before evening, if I know him."

"I hope so," Philippa said, and, kissing her father once more, she went to write to Don Fernando.

She had destroyed two unsatisfactory drafts of this awkward letter when the need for it was obviated.

"Don Fernando de Santiago y Anandas is waiting for you in the drawing-room," Jarvis told Philippa.

Philippa laughed and threw her third, half-finished draft into the waste-paper basket. She thanked Jarvis and said she would be down in a minute. She slowly tidied her hair. She had gone very white. "You jilted a man yesterday; you can do it today!" she told her reflection in the cheval-glass. Then she sighed and walked quickly downstairs.

"Don Fernando, I am glad you called," she said as she entered the drawing-room. "I was just writing you a note to tell you I must speak to you."

Don Fernando was standing with his back to the door, admiring the ring he had bought for her. He whirled around.

"I have come to present you with a slight token of my esteem. I am frightened so hasty a marriage is disappointing to you—perhaps this will make amends."

Philippa gasped as he showed her the monstrous diamond. "Don Fernando, I must tell you—I am so sorry, but—"

Don Fernando's face fell. "Is it that you do not like diamonds? I do regret it. Sapphires, perhaps?"

"No! No, I beg of you! I—Don Fernando, I'm horribly, abjectly sorry, but I can't marry you!"

"But my dear Miss Winslow, do not think I do not understand. All brides have these qualms, I am told. There is nothing to be worried about. I will take care of you forever. All is well, little Philippa."

"All is *not* well! I cannot marry you! I have—well, I've changed my mind!"

"It is the haste, then? I admit I am impatient. I have left my business affairs and home for far too long. I must return to Spain, but if you wish for a more elaborate ceremony, you could wait until the autumn, when I can return. Then you can be married in St. George's with all the *ton* present," he said soothingly.

"No! I do not wish ever to marry you, Don Fernando. I've made a ghastly, impetuous mistake. Please forgive me!"

Don Fernando's face changed, his eyes narrowing and his jaw tightening. "It is another man, is it not?"

"What makes you guess that?"

"I am not a fool, Miss Winslow. You are in love. Not with me. Not with your complacent Earl. He didn't know, did he? I know. I know who you're in love with."

Philippa was frightened by the harshness of his tone. She had taken a step back from him. One hand was pressed to her mouth in a curiously forlorn gesture. Don Fernando, his voice hard and threatening, continued.

"You're in love with Charles Staunton. All London's guessed that. But I want to hear it from your lips. Tell me, Philippa. You love Charles Staunton, don't you?"

"I fancy Miss Winslow would prefer to answer that question in a less public place," a cool voice said from the doorway. Lord Charles, riding crop still in hand and his clothes spattered with mud, leaned against the doorjamb. Robin clutched at his sleeve. Henry Francis, Isabella, and Clarissa crowded behind him.

"That is, of course, if she wants to bother with such an absurd inquiry," he calmly added.

Chapter Eighteen

Philippa stood transfixed for a moment. Then she ran across the room. She stopped and stood directly in front of Lord Charles.

"You lied to me."

Lord Charles nodded.

"I'm so glad."

Philippa threw her arms around his neck and kissed him rapturously. Henry Francis stepped past them to lead Don Fernando out of the room, but the Spaniard held his ground.

"I am waiting for an explanation, Miss Winslow," he said coldly.

Philippa looked round at her disgruntled suitor. "Of course I love Charles Staunton."

"So of course she can't marry you," Lord Charles put in.

"I see," said Don Fernando with a certain lack of grace. "Permit me to say I do not wish you joy. You will remember how you have treated me, and you will regret it! 'Though the world for this commend thee/Though it smile upon the blow/Even its praises must offend thee/Founded on another's woe'!"

"I say, that's hardly fair, Don Fernando," Philippa retorted. "I don't think the world is going to commend me in the least. Everyone will agree that I have behaved abominably and that you are the injured party."

"Lord Byron himself, my dear sir, recommends 'One long last sigh to love and thee/Then back to busy life again'" Lord Charles said affably.

Don Fernando bowed to Philippa. "Good day, ma'am," he said sharply. He walked out of the room, past the children, still holding the velvet jewelbox.

"Oh, dear," murmured Philippa. "I do feel so dreadful."

"Don't worry," Lord Charles advised her. "You were not wholly to blame."

"I should say not!" She extricated herself from his embrace. "Why, in God's name, did you tell me you had cheated at cards?"

Henry Francis took Robin firmly by the hand and pushed Isabella and Clarissa toward the door.

"But I don't want to go," Robin exclaimed. "I told you Philippa was in the drawing-room, didn't I? Jarvis wouldn't have let you and Lord Charles in!"

"I don't think Jarvis could have kept Lord Charles out," Henry Francis replied in some amusement. "But come, we'll leave them alone."

"Why did Lord Charles tell Philippa he had cheated at cards?" Clarissa demanded. "I want to know!"

Philippa turned around. "Out, brats!" she said without rancour. They sighed, but docilely started to go, just as there was a knock sounded on the front door. Jarvis, who had been hovering about the hallway, deeply intrigued by the day's events, let in Lady Helena and the Earl of Carlington.

"Good day, Henry Francis," Lady Helena said. "Is Philippa in the drawing-room?"

Without waiting for an answer, she strode past the children and Henry Francis, who was speechless. Lord Carlington mutely followed her into the drawing-room.

"My word!" he exclaimed as he crossed the threshold. "Charles, what the devil are you doing here?" He then recalled himself and muttered an apology for his profanity to Lady Helena.

"Philippa," Lady Helena said accusingly, "I was told you are marrying Don Fernando."

"It was a mistake, Helena," Philippa said quietly.

"I should like to know something about it!" Lord Carlington told her.

Lord Charles put his arm around Philippa, who was trembling.

"George, I don't know quite how to explain this to you," he said. "I—"

He was interrupted by his mother, who walked in through the open door with Sir Rupert.

"George, what Charles is trying to tell you is that he is betrothed, now, to Miss Winslow," she said coolly.

The Earl's eyes bulged. "But *Charles!* Helena brought me here because Philippa was marrying *Don Fernando!* I hadn't the slightest notion . . ."

"Neither had I," Lady Helena said severely. "Philippa, this is odious!"

"I am very sorry, my Lord. I've been intolerably foolish. But don't you see that we'd never suit?"

"Philippa's much too frivolous—not to say flighty—for you, George," Lord Charles told his brother. He put his hand on Carlington's arm. "I've been in love with her for weeks, George. I didn't say anything, I swear to you, until after she had broken your engagement. Then I thought I could in honour ask her if she cared at all for me."

"Is that why you broke our engagement, Philippa?" the Earl said soberly.

Philippa nodded. "Yes, it is. I should never have told you I would marry you. I'm sorry."

"And what about Don Fernando?" Lady Helena asked. "Philippa, you've become a heartless jilt."

"Lady Helena," Lord Charles said evenly, "I sincerely hope you do not intend to repeat that epithet . . . to anyone."

His words carried a distinct menace, and Lady Blawith spoke quickly.

"Of course she won't, Charles. George, you do see that you're well rid of Miss Winslow? She wouldn't do for you at all."

"That has been amply demonstrated in the last few days," the Earl said with dignity. "I bear you no grudge, Miss Winslow. Nor you, Charles. I am only glad we have had our eyes opened in time."

"Thank you, George," said Lord Charles. Philippa gave the Earl a shy smile.

"What I want to know is," said Clarissa, who was standing in the doorway, "why did Lord Charles tell Philippa he'd cheated at cards?"

The Earl's benign expression abruptly changed. The blood drained from his face. "Charles!" he gasped. "You didn't!"

"No, of course he didn't, dear," his mother assured him. "He merely said he did. And most noble it was!"

"I don't understand. Charles, you were cad enough to do *that* as well as steal my bride?"

Lord Charles stood very straight. "George, on my honour I swear to you that I—"

"There's no need for dramatics, my boy," Sir Rupert drawled. "I marked the card, if you must know, Carlington. Dashed sorry and all that. I needed money."

The children's jaws dropped, but Robin muttered to his sisters, "I told you someone cheated. The Earl thought it was *me!*"

Lord Carlington heard him. With unusual dignity, the Earl stooped and put his hand on Robin's shoulder. I am sorry for that. It was unfair." He turned to face the others. "And, Charles, I can only say—"

"Don't bother, George. It is I, after all, who owe you the greater apology."

"But why did you tell Philippa you had done it, Charles?" Lady Helena asked reasonably.

"I—I felt she might, er—"

Lady Blawith came to his rescue. "He did it because Philippa wouldn't marry Carlington if she thought her father had done it. She wouldn't want to spoil his career. And Charles thought she loved George."

"Oh, I see," Philippa said. "Charles, I'm overwhelmed." Tears glistened on her eyelashes.

"Good," Lord Charles replied promptly. "Stay that way." He put his arm around her waist and kissed her hair. She smiled up at him, rather tremulously.

Lord Carlington, Lady Helena saw with satisfaction, was not even watching this touching scene. He was glaring at Sir Rupert.

"Winslow, do you realise the enormity of your deed?" he demanded.

"My Lord, I am quite aware of it. I shall make some small amends by, er, sparing England my presence for some time."

"Do that. If you don't leave the country, I shall feel myself honour-bound to have you expelled from your clubs."

"Don't get so upset, George," Lady Helena said softly. "He's said he's going to leave. I'm sure Cousin Rupert won't do it again. You don't need to concern yourself with it."

"You will go abroad, Father?" Henry Francis said.

"As soon as Philippa's married," Sir Rupert answered cheerfully. "I'll stay with Adelaide."

"Oh, good!" said Lady Blawith warmly. "Do give her my love."

"I am glad," the Earl announced, "that I shall no be intimately associated with this family. It has been a narrow escape. My future might have been ruined!"

"Don't get into such a taking, George. It's not ruined at all. It's just as brilliant as it always was."

"Thank you, Helena. That is very kind of you." The Earl smiled at Lady Helena. "Perhaps we should leave This room seems extraordinarily crowded. And every thing has been happily settled. Will you let me show you home, Helena?"

Lady Helena smiled. "But of course."

The Earl crossed the room and slapped his brother on the back. "She's a charming girl, Charles. But you're quite right; we shouldn't suit. I do wish you joy. Philippa my dear, you'll be happy with Charles."

He shook hands with Philippa, rather awkwardly then took Lady Helena's arm and left the room.

Philippa looked up at Lord Charles with dancin eyes. "Do you suppose . . . ?" she asked mischievously.

"Yes, I do," he answered. "How nicely it works out!"

His mother agreed. "Yes, indeed," said Lady Blawith "Helena has been in love with George for years, althoug I don't suppose she knew it herself until his betrothal.

"And Helena will take excellent care of him," Philip pa said. "And how good she'll be as a politician's wife! I makes me feel much better to know that he has her."

" 'Man was not form'd to live alone,' eh, Philippa? Lord Charles teased.

"Wretch!" Philippa exclaimed. "Don't you ever quo Byron to me again!"

Lord Charles, disobeying her, murmured, " 'All word are idle/Words from me are vainer still,' " and kissed he

"Children, now you must leave!" Henry Francis sai "It's all been explained, and now we can leave Philip and Lord Charles alone."

The children grumbled, and Henry Francis gently pushed them.

"Don't bother with them, Henry. I'll take them out. For a drive, maybe. I shall miss them in Germany," Sir Rupert said to his astonished elder son, and he firmly ushered his three youngest children out of the room.

"Well," said Henry Francis to no one in particular, "this may have done Father good. I've never known him to take the children out before!"

Philippa turned around in Lord Charles's arms. "Oh, that reminds me. Lady Blawith, is it true that Cousin Adelaide and Father wanted to marry each other years ago? Mama told me that once. She said it was all very sad."

"So it was. Adelaide and Maria had to marry money, you know, and when the Graf von Lansdorfer offered for her, her parents browbeat poor Adelaide into accepting. Not that anyone could tell then how abominably he would treat her! And he refused to help the family very much at all. An odious man, he was. And Rupert met your mother, and married her, a year later. I liked her, Philippa, but Adelaide would have been a much better influence. She wouldn't have let Sir Rupert get into these disgraceful ways!"

"Perhaps Cousin Adelaide can reform him now," Philippa said.

"I think you may rely upon it!" Lady Blawith informed her. "An excellent idea, sending Rupert to Bonn. Quite the best thing. And I must be going."

Lady Blawith kissed Philippa. "God bless you, my dear. I'm so glad you're not making poor Adelaide's mistake." She smiled gaily. "Charles is almost as wealthy as Farlington, and he's much more amusing!"

"Mother, you embarrass me," Lord Charles said politely.

"After explaining to George why you had your arm

around his *fiancée,* nothing should ever embarrass you,"
Lady Blawith told her son.

She kissed him. "I'm so happy that you won't be
sailing to Antigua, my dear."

Henry Francis showed her out, popping his head in
the door of the drawing-room afterward merely to say, "I
wish you joy, too. Keep a close eye on her, Staunton."

"I intend to," Lord Charles replied.

Henry Francis shut the door. Lord Charles and
Philippa were beside each other on the sofa. Philippa
rested her head on Lord Charles's shoulder.

"Are you aware," she said softly, "that you haven't
asked me to marry you?"

"I should think one betrothal a day was enough."

"Not when it was with the wrong man."

"Well, then, Miss Winslow, will you do me the inestimable honour of accepting my hand in marriage?"

"If I don't," Philippa said, "everyone truly will think
me a heartless jilt."

"And rightly so."

"Then I have no choice. I suppose I must marry you,
Lord Charles." Philippa sighed and kissed his cheek.

His arms tightened around her. "My God, we
shouldn't be joking about it! When I think how close you
were to marrying another—"

"Two others," Philippa interjected.

"My darling, it is appalling to contemplate. You
could be married now to George. To George!"

"But I'm not," Philippa calmly answered. "And
wouldn't be. I'm sure I would have realised my foolishness in time, even if I hadn't met you."

"I wish I could believe that! Although I must say
George took it better than I thought he would. He was
greatly disillusioned when you caused such a scene at
Almack's!"

"He's well rid of me," Philippa said thoughtfully.
"The Duke of Hetford's probity is unquestioned."

Lord Charles looked at her sharply; her tone was bitter.

"Charles," she said, "tell me truly: does it bother you? My father?"

"Don't let that trouble you, dearest. I know George would mind, but I couldn't care less. I like your disreputable father almost as much as your virtuous brother. Without them, my dear, you'd be marrying Don Fernando this afternoon."

Philippa shuddered. "We were lucky. Just like a novel: everything working out right in the last chapter."

"Isabella will be pleased."

"You're too prosaic a hero for her tastes, though. No black mustachios, no dark secret—or so I hope. There's nothing truly dashing about you at all!"

"How can you say that, you ungrateful minx, when I had you convinced I was a rogue and a spendthrift, and when I've stolen a bride from under two far more worthy gentlemen's noses?"

"True enough," Philippa said. "I should have known you for a scoundrel the first time I met you!"

"You certainly formed a disfavourable opinion of me. Very quickly!"

"I suppose so. Charles, you keep horses of your own stabled on the road to Wimcombe and Oxford, don't you?"

"Yes, Philippa."

"So I shall never again have to wait in that innyard for posthorses, will I?"

"Never again."

"What a pity."

Philippa heaved a sigh. Lord Charles, undeceived, shook her.

"After all, my dear," he told her solemnly, "you never know whom you might meet."

Philippa opened her mouth to retort, but Lord Charles swiftly kissed her. Philippa found herself quite unable to remember what it was she had meant to say.

ROMANTIC SUSPENSE
FROM DOROTHY DANIELS

MIRROR OR SHADOWS   (92-149, $2.25)
by Dorothy Daniels

nly women descended from the Irish Queen
aeve were able to see the visions in the ancient
irror. Beautiful Maeve O'Hanlon cherished it.
its pale lustre she saw not only the face of the
an she would marry, but a vision of the danger
e would face as well.

PERRINE by Dorothy Daniels   (82-605, $2.25)

hen the beautiful Perrine fled the gypsy camp
ere she was raised, she knew only that she
uld not bear to wed the violent man to whom
e was betrothed. She did not dream that he
uld follow her across two continents, haunt-
g her, sworn not to rest until he saw her in her
ave!

THE MAGIC RING   (82-789, $2.25)
by Dorothy Daniels

e magic ring — a lucky ring — was a gift from
ross the seas from the parents whom Angela
d not seen since their return to Italy ten years
fore. Angela slipped it on her finger and made
promise to herself. She would find her parents
ce again, even if she had to defy the secret
cieties that held Italy in terror, even if she
ust risk her very life.